The Wonder-Worker

Books by Dan Jacobson

The Trap
A Dance in the Sun
The Price of Diamonds
The Zulu and the Zeide (*Stories*)
Evidence of Love
No Further West (*Memoir*)
Time of Arrival and Other Essays
The Beginners
Through the Wilderness and Other Stories
The Rape of Tamar
The Wonder-Worker

The
Wonder-Worker

by Dan Jacobson

An Atlantic Monthly Press Book
Little, Brown and Company • Boston • Toronto

Fund-Title II-A

FIRST AMERICAN EDITION

Library of Congress Cataloging in Publication Data

Jacobson, Dan.
  The wonder-worker.

  "An Atlantic Monthly Press book."
  I. Title.
PZ4.J175Wo3 [PR9369.3.J3]   823'.9'12   73-20406
ISBN 0-316-45562-8

ATLANTIC–LITTLE, BROWN BOOKS
ARE PUBLISHED BY
LITTLE, BROWN AND COMPANY
IN ASSOCIATION WITH
THE ATLANTIC MONTHLY PRESS

PRINTED IN THE UNITED STATES OF AMERICA

The annunciation. On the night Timothy Fogel was conceived, his mother yelled out so loudly she was heard in distant rooms.

She had not been raped. Nor was she crying out in a fit of contrition. She had been quite willing to let her husband approach her; and then broach her. Subsequently, as on previous, unremarkable occasions, he fell off her, she rolled over, they lay drowsing together in a muddle of warmth, slipperiness, hairiness, nakedness, niceness, etcetera.

All this took place on a hired bed, in a hired room, on the Isle of Wight. They had come to the resort of Ventnor to breathe its sea air, to walk on its cliff tops, to sit in the chintzy parlour of one of its boarding houses, and to stroke the sluggish black cats who lodged there permanently. And they had also come, though neither of them knew it at the time, to summon Timothy into existence.

Maureen Fogel's scream woke her up from the doze into which she had fallen; it woke up almost everyone in the boarding house. Gerhard responded instinctively by grappling with the creature he found in his bed, and clapping his hand across its mouth. Maureen gulped, shivered, began to cry in a childish manner. Already, there were scufflings, as of slippers on linoleum, outside the door of their room, and the sound of voices whispering together in anxious consultation.

Finally, a genteel knock sounded upon the door, and a voice called out, 'Is anything the matter?'

The owner of that voice was a particularly odious man: the father of a family that lived in a couple of rooms down the passage. He was a smiler at strangers, an organiser of outings, a wearer of a navy-blue blazer with gilt buttons; he walked with a curious, forward-sloping scurry, like a department-store supervisor, yet he affected the language and airs of a military man. Just the one, in other words, to be first on the scene after a woman's screams had pierced the silence of the night; to call the police and an ambulance; to note down the names and addresses of all potential witnesses; to make sure that nothing was done that might disarrange any clues left behind by the murderer.

But he was given no opportunity to display his many talents that evening. Standing stark naked in the darkness between the door and his snivelling wife, Gerhard called out in the most sincere and most

English voice he could summon up for the occasion that really nothing was wrong, truly so, his wife had had a nightmare, he was sorry for the disturbance she had caused.

There were a few more shufflings outside, further whispers and exclamations, and a final, desultory exchange of messages through the door. The relief party began to disperse. Gerhard returned to his side of the bed and switched on the bedside lamp. He and Maureen scrambled into their respective sets of nightclothes. He switched off the lamp. She whispered incoherently to him. She couldn't remember what had happened – that scream had woken her up – she'd thought it was someone else screaming, like all the devils of hell were after him – she'd be so ashamed in front of all the others the next morning, with their great staring eyes – nothing like it had ever come over her before – everything dark and still, and then that wicked noise . . .

She whispered, he slept, young Timothy consolidated himself where he was, and promptly began to grow.

His advent was thus accompanied by omens. Within the moist, lightless crevices of Maureen Fogel's organs of generation, two minuscule germs came together, and the result was that her entire system was convulsed with terror and wonder. As well it might be. But neither she nor Gerhard had any inkling of the significance of her cry. Nine months had to pass before they were to be enlightened. The next morning they discussed whether Maureen had perhaps eaten something that had disagreed with her, or whether it was just the strangeness of her surroundings that had made her yell out like that. They came to no conclusion. There was none for them to come to. They greeted the guests at breakfast apologetically, and ate their bacon and eggs while the others surreptitiously examined Maureen for signs of the beating which they assumed Gerhard had given her. The gentleman in the navy-blue blazer nodded understandingly at him, over his pot of tea, and in return was rewarded with a craven, man-of-the-world smile. During the week that remained to the Fogels in Ventnor none of the other guests in the boarding house ever referred to the matter. Nor did their landlady. Gerhard noticed, however, that when they left she did not give them the souvenir ashtray, with a map of the island printed in colour upon it, that was formally presented to all the other departing guests. They had not been forgiven.

For the rest it was a quiet holiday. Both Maureen and Gerhard were to have pleasant memories of Ventnor in the early spring. The boarding house was in the upper part of the town, where many similar, slate-roofed establishments kept it company, along with a surprising number of spiritualist chapels and fish and chip shops. Between them and the cavernous Edwardian hotels on the seafront were the unalarming cliffs. Asphalted paths zig-zagged up and down, children gingerly lowered their tubular, overcoated bodies on to the damp turf and their mothers stooped to pick them up, old men sat on benches. Beyond was a rather pallid sea, much traversed by boats of all sizes heading in and out of Southampton.

In the evening the sun set over the sea, and then its colours became more various and animated, it shone like the neck of a glossy tropical bird. Maureen and Gerhard walked, they watched the children playing, they boated on the artificial pond in the municipal pleasure ground. It was a holiday like any other. Gerhard read. He sketched a little. Maureen sat beside him, doing nothing. She had a great gift for doing nothing. For thinking about nothing. For feeling nothing. Apart from that one wholehearted, involuntary scream she remained as blank, as splendidly open to disregard, as the sea itself on its calmest days. So Gerhard ignored her. As he usually did. As she expected him to.

Then they went back to London. All continued as before. Gerhard did his work. Maureen went every day to Robinson's newsagency and tobacco shop where he had found her almost five years before.

From his upstairs window, looking down the slope of the hill, Gerhard took in the view of many roofs of slate and tile, clambering upon one another like heaps of shamelessly mating crustaceans. The prospect was one he had painted often, though never to his entire satisfaction. Even to his uncritical eye it seemed that he hadn't once quite got the sense of grapple. Now, for reasons that had more to do with economy than with art, he decided that the light from the overcast sky was good enough for him to work by.

He was doing a sign for a woman who was opening a secretarial and employment bureau in the main road nearby. It was a straightforward commission.

9

Name of bureau and (in brackets below) name of proprietress. Plain black Roman lettering, on a white background. 18″ × 12″. But there was some scope for artistic initiative in the clenched hand, with one finger pointing heavenward, that the woman wanted to appear in the corner of the board, so that it would be clear to everyone that the office was upstairs. Should the hand be viewed from the front or back? Should it be given that florid cuff of conjoined circles which printers are so fond of? Or amputated mercilessly at the wrist, like that of a victim of an industrial accident? Or perhaps it should be a woman's delicate hand, with long, oval fingernails? Gerhard sketched out all these possibilities, and eventually decided on an ordinary, businessman's hand and cuff.

The morning passed peacefully. The sounds that penetrated his studio, formerly a back bedroom, were those of a Thursday. There was the melancholy, off-key, five-note howl of the rag and bone man: *Enny-o-eye-booOW*. Then another weekly visitor: the municipal street sweeping cart, a monstrous roaring affair of barrels, brushes, and corrugated suction pipes of gross bore, like a howitzer's. Other, diurnal sounds marked the passing of the hours. The milk-cart clopped and clashed down the road. 10 a.m. The children at school some blocks away came out for their playtime and promptly began cheering and screaming, as if at the progress of a king among them. With the same suddenness as it had begun (Gerhard couldn't hear the school bell) the noise was cut off some minutes later. The children raised that clamour every school day, always with the same passionate, incomprehensible enthusiasm. 11 a.m. Time for tea.

The room was heated by a black, chimney-shaped oil stove on splayed metal paws, and Gerhard put the kettle on to boil simply by placing it on top of the stove, though he knew one was not supposed to do it. But he had been doing it for a long time. For years.

Later the greengrocer's boy swore that he had been banging and kicking as hard as he could for minutes on end at the front door; and when he saw him, with his disordered hair and accusing eyes, Gerhard had to believe him. On the other hand, the house was so small he couldn't understand how he could have failed to hear the noise. He suspected the boy must have been knocking at the door of the next house up or down. It was difficult to tell one from another along Omdurman Terrace. They all had pointed, vaguely ecclesiastical little porches in front, and dwarfish, befoliated pilasters of stucco decorating their downstairs bay windows. At intervals tunnels were run through the terrace to give access to the gardens at the back.

Anyway, Gerhard stood in his room listening for the sound of which he had become aware only after it had stopped. He went down the stairs, past the hall-stand, and opened the front door. No-one there. The terrace, running uphill to the shops, and downhill into a bird's-foot junction with several other streets, was deserted. Trees held out their bare branches quite still, showing that they had nothing to conceal. Gerhard shut the door and went back to his studio. For some reason he crossed to the window. In the middle of his garden was a small, sodden patch of green. In the middle of that, semaphoring with both arms, stood a white-coated figure whose face was familiar to Gerhard, though he could not have said from where. He opened the window.

'It's your wife!' the boy shouted. 'Something's happened to her. She's very poorly. You must come at once. You're already late. I've been knocking and knocking.'

Gerhard was sure he had the wrong man. He had not been knocking on *his* door; he would have heard him. His wife was never taken poorly. There was nothing he could be late for; not the way he lived. So more time was lost while Gerhard established the boy's identity, and then made sure that it was really he who was wanted. Then, finally, he ran. Up the hill to the shops.

He was not too late.

Between his wife's legs, surrounded by the gingery fleece of her own hairs, was a darker patch, a gleaming shadow, in the shape of an ellipse.

Electric lights burned overhead. Time passed.

The ellipse grew broader. It had the shape of a rugby ball. Like the hardest, earliest bud of spring, it was gripped tight by sepals composed of fold upon fold of unyielding flesh. Gerhard held Maureen's hand. She did not appear to recognise him. Her head was turned to one side, with a pillow beneath it. Her legs were retracted. She lay on the floor of the shop; there was a blanket beneath her, and beneath that what looked like an entire day's supply of the *Mirror* and the *Sketch*. The little shop was full of people: Mrs Robinson, two ambulance men who had come too late to move the patient, and whose vehicle was parked outside, a midwife summoned from who knew where, the woman from the greengrocery next door.

Mr Robinson stood in the door at the back of the shop, keeping a distance between himself and the indelicacies taking place on the floor. Whenever he caught Gerhard's eye he coughed discreetly and fixed upon him a look of reproach for allowing such a thing to happen to his wife, and especially so during business hours. The front door to the shop had been closed and the window blinds pulled down.

Maureen sweated. Sometimes she cried out. Her face was sculptured by strain, ennobled by it. The gentle depressions on both sides of her nose had become deep furrows, her eyes were lost in their sockets, the corners of her pallid mouth were bent down like the ends of a bow. Elsewhere, at a distance her body alone seemed incapable of bridging, other changes were taking place. The sepals were beginning to yield. The bud within them throbbed and broadened, throbbed and rested, broadened again, perceptibly pushing itself forward. From one moment to the next it ceased to be a bud and became fruit-like. Streaks of black lay upon its surface, with the look of grass trapped down by water. Maureen showed her teeth and the whites of her eyes. Between her thighs there was growing a small, round, human head that, unlike hers, made no sound. Who could believe what he saw? Out of the same cavity – while Maureen's face contracted and expanded into snarls and grins, or composed itself into spells of what looked like cogitation – there now grew a tiny lilac-coloured arm, complete with fingers at the end of it. Maureen sighed and a second arm appeared. This one was grazed with blood. Both had a collapsed, fleshless appearance. They came together in a gesture of supplication.

Then, slithering out in haste, as if out of some kind of emergency rescue apparatus, the whole baby was there. A single, perfect lilac in hue, he lay against Maureen's leg. From his little belly there protruded a disproportionately large umbilical cord, gleaming white, hung about with other cords of other colours, all twining back to the open, pulsing cavern, with blood-flecked hair around it, from which everything had come. The baby was scooped up. He gave a small cough, more like someone clearing a frog in his throat than a cry. Gerhard thought he heard himself roaring with relief, and found he was merely wiping his eyes on the back of his hand, in silence, ignored for the moment by the others.

Of what happened next he was to retain only a memory of a profusion of colours. There was some bright red blood and some dark. There were veins of lavender, of pink, and the palest blue. There was a bag of purple and rust that was promptly wrapped up in newspaper and put out of sight. There were whites that gleamed like mother-of-pearl, blank whites, blue whites, whites marbled lavishly with mauve. The baby's lilac colour was fading rapidly to a commonplace grey. Eventually he was swaddled in a sheet and put next to Maureen on the ambulance stretcher. The door was opened. Outside, the wan light of a December noon seemed unreal, it had so much tall space to fill, it had to spread itself so thin. A group of smiling, craning people, through whom Maureen had to be carried to get to the ambulance, had gathered on the pavement. The whole world knew already. It would be in the papers that evening: *Baby Born in Newsagent's Shop*. Gerhard was afraid he would be cheered or booed when he went out. Mr Robinson stood at the door, while some industrious cleaning up took place within. He shook Gerhard's hand and breathed heavily at him, but said nothing in reply to the incoherent thanks and apologies Gerhard stammered out. He managed to make his getaway, clutching a few items of blood-stained clothing that had been bundled up in newspaper. He went down the street, expecting to be called back at any moment, as if he had just committed a crime. He walked like a man imitating a man walking.

No-one called him back. Instead, a couple of blocks further down, he was summoned forward by the sight of another group of people standing together on the pavement, half-way down the slope of the street. They were opposite his house. One man ran up to the group; others were pointing upwards; someone else ran away. Gerhard quickened his pace, trying to see what they were so excited about.

There appeared to be nothing out of the ordinary for them to be staring at. Then he saw a languid coil of smoke emerge from under the eave of his house. The smoke lay against the plaster and brickwork of the eave like an animal reluctant to come out of its shelter, before it slowly crept over the guttering. Hand over hand, it began feeling its way up the slates of the roof.

The paraffin stove! The kettle! Trapped by the kettle, the hot air within the stove must have exploded, scattering burning oil everywhere. Gerhard saw it all in an instant. Without reflection or hesitation, he put his head down, turned up his coat collar, lifted the bundle he was carrying to shoulder height,

15

so that it concealed his face, and passed the group on the pavement with the air of a preoccupied stranger.

A windy blue and white sky outside. The pine trees sway and plunge in unison, like the members of an orchestra, as they make their sounds together. The lake is more ruffled than I've seen it before. Birds fly in groups beneath my window, across the valley; they twitch their wings and glide, then twitch them again in a little spasm. There is something toy-like and mechanical about the irregularity of their movements; but they go where they please, and are soon lost, indistinguishable from the tiny specks and lines that always flaw one's vision when one stares directly into the sky.

Now I look at the picture on the wall of this room. It's just a piece of hotel furniture, nothing more. A water colour of some kind, with a peculiar glaze upon it: you might almost think it's been coated in egg-white and then put into an oven and baked, like a loaf of home-made bread. It shows a field at sunset, with old-fashioned stooks of wheat in the foreground and a vague house, fence, and tree in the background. All very conventional. The stooks are aflame in the light of the sun; smudged with black and red, they rise like bonfires from the yellow stubble. The artist hasn't put his name to the picture; out of a just shame, I'd like to believe, at the mediocrity of what he has produced.

OK. A picture. A representation. A poor one too. But imagine that *in* that picture you choked, you burned, you were heaped up and dissipated like flame, your fingertips stiffened and charred in the heat. Nothing would change. You could not move. The sun that had never risen, but had always been there, would never set.

That's the nearest I can come to describing what happened to me. A visitation. I sat here, trapped in the lives I was writing about, unable to shift myself out of them, or to shift from myself the conviction that they belong to me. Gerhard! Maureen! Timothy! At best they're caricatures, cartoons, cheap satiric spooks and might-have-beens. I can see through them. I can see who they are parodying. I may be in a bad way, in need of a rest, 'ill', I may have made a balls-up of many things. But I'm not a complete fool. Or a tool. I still have a life of my own.

Now the picture hangs harmlessly in its frame. I'm in possession of myself once more. The pile of papers lies on my desk, where I left it. I wait for the doctor to arrive. Everything is again in order.

Some further particulars of Timothy's conception, birth, and infancy have to be mentioned, it seems, at this point.

1. On the night of Timothy's conception, Gerhard and Maureen had been married for one thousand five hundred and fifty-four days: that is, just twice seven hundred and seventy-seven. It was also the thirty-third day after Maureen's thirty-third birthday. Nine months later Timothy was born, on the ninety-ninth day before the eleventh anniversary of Gerhard's arrival in England.

These and several other calculations were made on scraps of paper and on the backs of envelopes by Gerhard, while he waited for the rebuilding of the fire-gutted first storey of his house.

2. Timothy was born under the sign of the Goat.

3. His name was chosen for him by his mother. On consulting a dictionary of proper names, Gerhard established that the name was of Greek origin and signified 'fearing or honouring God'.

4. Maureen had remained ignorant of Timothy's presence inside her throughout her pregnancy. When doctors and nursing staff at the maternity hospital asked her how she had managed it, she answered that she *had* thought there was 'something strange going on', but had been afraid it was a growth of some kind. So she hadn't dared to ask a doctor about it. Also, she confessed, she got 'all muddled up' with her dates every month.

Gerhard excused himself by saying that his wife was so big and the baby so small, it could easily have hidden inside her. He also said he wasn't in the habit of studying his wife's figure every morning; he had more interesting things to look at. Anyway, after one thousand five hundred days of childless marriage, a baby was the last thing he would have expected her to start up all of a sudden.

5. When Gerhard first saw the baby in his little white cot, he studied him carefully for some time before remarking: 'At least he doesn't look like Mr Truter.'

Later he made a tour of the ward, inspecting all the other babies in their cots and the recently depleted mothers in their beds. 'A *lot* of the other babies look like Mr Truter,' he reported emphatically at the end of his tour.

6. Though he observed none of the commandments of Jewish religious law, Gerhard insisted that Timothy

be circumcised. 'It's for the sake of his looks,' he explained earnestly to Maureen. 'Instead of a kind of pointed worm growing down there, he'll have a nice round thing, like a little acorn. I can remember the difference from when I was a boy at school.'

Accordingly, after the baby had reached the weight of six pounds, the operation was carried out in entirely secular fashion by a member of the hospital staff. Timothy cried fiercely at the time, and for several days afterwards broke into fresh howls every time he had to do a pee.

7. Timothy resisted successfully all Maureen's early attempts to wean him. Even after his first birthday, when he already had several shining white teeth in his head, the sight of her breast over his cot made him stretch out his arms excitedly and arch his entire body upwards, until it was supported only by the back of his head and the back of his heels. Each time his mouth finally found Maureen's upright, rufous nipple, a thrill ran through his small frame; then he lay motionless for a while, his mouth full, his jaws idle, his nose embedded in her soft flesh. He would always wait in this manner, eyelids lowered with an air of calculation, before beginning to drink; once he had begun he went on steadily, for as long as he was allowed to, interrupting himself only to utter certain greedy yet reflective sighs.

8. When she was discharged from the maternity hospital, Maureen and her baby had to go initially into a hostel run by the welfare department of the Borough of Hornsey. There was nowhere else for them to go, since the damage done by fire and water to the house in Omdurman Terrace had not yet been

made good.

All the negotiations over the repair of the house were conducted by Gerhard with Mr Truter, who was employed by a local firm of estate agents, who in turn acted on behalf of the ancient ecclesiastical institution that owned all of Omdurman Terrace and many surrounding terraces like it.

During this period, and subsequently while the builders were in the house, Gerhard camped downstairs in the living room.

9. On at least four occasions he quietly walked out of his encampment downstairs with the intention of never returning to it, leaving behind him no indication where he had gone. He was brought back every time by the thought of the uncanny powers that his child had already displayed, both in concealing and in revealing himself. You could never tell where they might strike next.

Timothy started to walk late. His vocabulary, by the time he reached his second birthday, was smaller than that of most other children of his age, and he relied heavily on various grunts and emphatic manners of pointing. He still had to wear napkins and rubber pants at all times. He was no good at assembling his blocks and beakers into towers, and hadn't even begun to scribble with the crayons which his father was forever pushing hopefully into his hand.

Physically, however, he was well developed. He shone. Every square inch of his skin had its own special gleam or glitter; not to speak of his hair, his teeth, his fingernails, or his light brown eyes. (Almost orange they were, in the sunlight.) His skin was as soft as blossom, his limbs were as pliable as clay. The pink outer flesh of his lips looked even more tender than the tongue and membranes inside them. Despite his plumpness, his hips were slim, recognisably a boy's, and his bottom was pointed. From his head (whose disproportionate size made him appear to belong already to the adult world, only better, fresher, cleaner, less flawed) he tapered like a fish to narrow feet and inconsequential toes, as round as little Chinese bells.

The shrivelled infant had gone, taking with him all his jerking, uncoordinated arm and leg movements; so had the staring six-month-old, startlingly fat, inflated with Maureen's milk, unable to pick himself up or to crawl and therefore compelled to lie helplessly on his back, as vibrant with unreleased potentialities as a small power station or a large queen ant. Gone too was the smudged crawler, the careful, intricate riser to his feet and unsteady balancer upon them, the staggerer of his first few paces, the self-applauding collapser on to his own padded bottom; gone all the sounds that each of these avatars of Timothy had produced, from the plasm-rending cries of early infancy to the elaborate speech-like babblings that had been aired before words finally came. They had all been shouldered not only out of existence in the present, but even out of the recollections of his parents. At every stage he had completely and mysteriously taken the place of himself, so that nothing but what he now was appeared ever to have been, both in his own apprehensions and in those of the people around him.

So goes the law of childhood. And parenthood.

Obedient to it still, Timothy accompanies his father on the walk they take at that hour every Friday afternoon. Gerhard wheels an empty push-chair in front of him; Timothy himself is attached to the other side of it by one gloved hand. He is wearing a girl's fluffy pink coat bought second-hand for him; on his head is a knitted woollen cap, with an unravelling weed-like pom-pom on top of it, which Maureen is soon to snip off altogether, only to find that the entire cap will then begin to unwind from the centre outwards. Other, much graver misfortunes lie farther ahead; none of them can be discerned by either Timothy or Gerhard, who screw up their eyes at the dazzling silver reflections that stretch forward and contract like lashes around every damp patch on the pavement. After a day of quiet periods of drizzle, and even quieter periods of waiting for the drizzle to start again, the sun has taken its last chance to appear, just a few feet above the horizon.

As always, Timothy and Gerhard make their way to the park nearest their house: a space of green turf and a few trees surrounded entirely by the backs of houses. In the middle of it stands a metal gibbet from which several swings hang on chains; a merry-go-round in the shape of one of those cages in which Jews and felons were once suspended from church towers; and a heavily-skirted, cast-iron battlehorse with half a dozen seats and hand-holds ranged along its back. Timothy runs straight to this group of playthings, and climbs on to the foremost of the seats on the horse's back. With both hands he holds on to the metal pipes that protrude out of the animal's ears ; he leaves the rest to his father.

24

Gerhard does what is expected of him. He rocks the horse up and down. Caught between fear and pleasure, Timothy doesn't dare to look anywhere but directly in front of him, lest even a movement of his eyes be sufficient to unbalance him and throw him to the ground two feet below. There is a set smile on his lips. He breathes in snatches only. Finally he says, ' 'Top – get off now – 'nuff !' and when the heavy horse is brought to a halt and he is lifted off it, he feels as relieved as he will years later on leaving aeroplanes at the end of long journeys. Gerhard consults his watch. It is only four-thirty. He cannot start for home yet.

Timothy then sits in one of the swings that has a small, box-like frame around it. Surrounded to the height of his chest by the wooden bars, he feels more secure than he had felt on the horse, and he leans forward and lets his head hang over the top bar. His father pushes him gently. He appears to fall asleep; only an intermittent flicker of his eyelashes above his round cheeks shows that he is still awake. Gerhard consults his watch once more; he bends down and studies Timothy's half-concealed face, to see if he can find in it any resemblance to the briskly assembled features of Mr Truter. As he has done innumerable times before, he comes up convinced that there is no such resemblance.

'Want mama.'

'In a little while.'

'Want mama now.'

'In a little while.'

The swing rocks gently. Timothy rests against the bars. A little time goes by. And a little more. It is still

Friday afternoon. Timothy is now three years old. Another Friday. Timothy is four. Now he sits on a swing with no bars around it, and he holds on to its chains on both sides of him; he works the swing by pulling his legs in and stretching them high in the air in front of him. He wears blue corduroy trousers and sandals; his coat is of leather, in a style fashionable at the time, and he has a matching leather cap.

'What's the time, papa?'

'Nearly five o'clock.'

'Is mummy finished with Mr Truter now?'

'I think she must be, yes, Timothy.'

With each question Timothy has swept forward; each reply sends him away in a reverse arc through the air.

'Then let's go home.'

'In a little while.'

Timothy's attention is distracted from his father by the approach of a little girl in a brown dress, who has been unsuccessfully trying to get the iron rocking-horse to move beneath her, while at the same time loudly forbidding her mother to come to her help. She is about the same age as Timothy. Her hair is tied into two bunches which stick out sideways, one over each ear; as a result a tight path runs down the flattened back of her head, which Timothy is able to view from the peaks of his journeys back and forth.

'Careful, Susie,' the girl's mother calls out from behind the hooded, laden pram she is pushing. The girl sidles closer to the swings. Timothy is at once impelled to work his legs up and down more vigorously than before. Looking up at him, the girl captures one of the box-like swings and climbs into it.

26

'Baby swing,' says Timothy, as if into the air, while he flies past her.

He is right. The swing is so small the girl has much difficulty getting into it. Once there, she begins to work her legs slowly, making no attempt to compete with him. But she keeps her eyes on him. He knows she's watching. The two parents stand uncomfortably side by side, drawn willy-nilly into association with one another. Neither of them speaks. Timothy lets his swing slow down until it is hardly moving. Then he shifts the grip of his hands on the chains, and the grip of his bottom on the wood beneath it. He brings his knees to his chest and puts his heels on the wooden seat. He is about to do something he has long wanted to do, but has not yet dared to try. The moment for it has arrived, now that the little girl is gazing on admiringly. Gingerly, holding fast to the chains, looking neither at his father nor at the girl, but only at the peaked, meat-coloured roofs of red and black on the far side of the park, he lifts himself up and stands on the seat of the swing. His knees are still bent cautiously, his bottom protrudes behind. But it is well clear of the wood; he is undeniably on his feet.

He stands for a moment only. As he begins to lower himself, the swing slithers away. Just a few inches. Enough. His whole body is electrified; it lurches, clutches, his spine dazzles, his mind is put out. He hangs upside down, roaring with fright. The shock of the world is upon him.

He sees how it is. It is other. It does not yield. It is magnified and black. It shines from myriad points of light. It has seams upon it, like the wrinkles on an aged face. A small round stone, rolled there from starlike distances, rests upon it. There is pain, there is noise somewhere; both pain and noise are his, Timothy's, yet he is not where they are. Rather, he is at the gates of the implacable silence and insentience revealed to him. Tiny, they are spacious. Motionless, they are charged with power. Impenetrable, they offer him their sovereign peace. Indifferent, they have always waited for him.

Then all of it is snatched away from him. Hands pull him through the air and paddle uncertainly at him. A strange woman says, 'What a brave little lad!' A girl whose hair is tied in two pig-tails looks at him with distress and satisfaction as she swings slowly back and forth in a small wooden cage. His father's anxious face is barely two inches from his own. There are rimless, polygonal pieces of glass in front of Gerhard's eyes. Elastic, whitish patches of moisture are huddled into the corners of his mouth; minuscule bubbles in them wink as his lips move, uttering distraught words of endearment and comfort.

How long had Timothy been away? How long had he hung upside down, his face on the ground? Later, the footsteps of his memory could always find their way back to that park, but they could never go beyond or behind the moment when the sky reeled back into place, his father loomed over him, and he, snatched away from what had been revealed to him, cried as much out of a sense of deprivation as of relief.

On the whole, I can't complain. Perhaps Dr Wuchs's treatments are more effective than I'm prepared to allow. The place must have something to do with it, too. Mountain air and pine forests up here; museums, cathedrals and picturesque *Viertel* in the city down there – not to mention a lake – with a black Mercedes limousine shuttling back and forth every thirty minutes. Excellent food; secluded gravelled walks through the woods; a swimming-bath set among lawns and rose beds; tastefully furnished public rooms; a view in the mornings and evenings, when the air is at its clearest, of snow-capped mountains on the horizon; a terraced garden where little waterfalls, hung about by aromatic shrubs, tinkle musically night and day – what more could I have hoped for? I'd even say it's worth the money they must be charging for it all, if I knew of any way of measuring what such luxuries are really worth. One of the earliest surprises of wealth, for me, was to realise that places like these make you pay through the nose for the opportunity they give you of showing that you can afford their charges!

The guests are all pretty long in the tooth. Inevitably, given the kind of establishment it is. Germans and Americans abound. Also inevitably. The Americans don't seem to stay for more than a few days, exchanging notes about where they have been or where they are going next. The Germans stay longer. Many of the Americans are Jews. Many of the more decrepit Germans are old enough to have been Jew-killers. Now they sit side by side at tables in the dining room, with its great curved windows looking out over the pine-covered slopes, and they stuff themselves with goodies of all kinds. Neutral Switzerland! Neutral money! Neutral luxury! *Wunderbar!*

For dinner last night one of the old Germans had a pound of raw, minced flesh, into which a trio of white-coated flunkeys broke raw eggs, sprinkled salt, pepper, and chopped-up parsley, poured glasses of Burgundy and cups of milk. Then he spooned up the entire mess, without much relish, dutifully as it were, no doubt hoping to feel a manly vigour surging back into his balls even while he sat there. I suspect he must be under the supervision of someone like Dr Wuchs. If not of Dr Wuchs himself. That would be a laugh. But I wouldn't put it past the good, grey, money-grubbing doctor. To me he says: eat little meat, avoid animal proteins in general, keep away from alcohol, avoid spices. To my German friend he says: *steak tartare* for you, *mein Herr*, with plenty of eggs, milk and Burgundy thrown in, and just see the difference it will make. To both of us he gives his famous course of injections, and puts to us his searching questions about the vicissitudes of our past and our goals for the future. 'Psycho-physical equilibrium' he promises us, if we submit to his treatments and try sincerely to follow his advice. All for a fee, of course. Again, you must pay for the privilege of showing that you can afford to join the select group of eminent people whose names the doctor lets fall from his lips from time to time: General X, *Minister-präsident* Y, Cardinal Z. And, of course, my so-charming, so-gifted papa, at whose recommendation Dr Wuchs naturally assumes me to be here.

Why not? I have nothing to lose. At the end of every session with me he fills his syringe with a mix from various little bottles which he takes out of his bag, and shoots it into my bum. I sleep. For all I know he may be turning me into a junkie. (Hence those 'memoirs'? *This?*) I wake up to the afternoon light streaming past my window. All calm and comfortable. When I go to the window I see the blue, wrinkled surface of the lake, many miles below, with triangular sails moving at random across it. The sails are too small at this distance to have any colour. Around the water are gathered many domes and steeples, modern buildings in beige or bottle-green, villas with pitched roofs that look from up here like so many books opened and stood spine upwards to dry after a ducking. On the crests of the tree-clad mountains on the far side are various radio

31

and electricity masts. From where I stand it all appears idyllically silent and peaceful: a model city, model lake, model mountains, a model view.

But I'm not being a model patient. Dr Wuchs says so. He says I'm not really being cooperative enough. I must answer his questions less – less – how shall he put it? – not so – erratically. Otherwise the pills and injections he gives me will lose much of their efficacy. I ask him to tell me why. He obliges. He has a large, loose, earnest, aged face; on his lower lip there is a sore place, a small depression, whitish in colour, with a pustulent look. When he falls silent the tip of his tongue appears and comes to rest briefly on that ulcer, giving it a slightly anxious, surreptitious dab. Then he finds the English word he has paused to look for, and continues as fluently as before. He tells me about the vitally important difference between vitamin supplements from organic sources and those which are produced artificially. About the trace elements (iron, gold, phosphorus, God knows what) which he introduces at certain times and in certain places in the systems of his patients. About the hormones he obtains for the same purpose from freshly slaughtered chickens, sheep, and rhesus monkeys. About the state of 'self-understanding' *(Selbstverstehen)* at which his patients should arrive if they are to draw the fullest possible benefit from the substances he puts into them. For if the patient is not ready mentally and emotionally for the physical aspects of the treatment, he explains, then there is likely to take place in his system a certain – er – ahm – *Zusammenziehung*. That is to say, contraction and rejection. Speaking chemically, I must understand. On the cellular level, the level of the basic life-unit, and of the molecules of which it is composed. He is not using metaphors, he is not speaking like a literary gentleman, but as a scientist, whose only concern is with what exists objectively in the world. Objectively, the self exists. Subjectivity exists. Why take fright, scientifically speaking, at so old a conundrum? Everyone knows nowadays that stomach ulcers, cardiac crises, asthma, skin ailments, rheumatism, even cancers and tuberculosis, are what people are pleased to call 'psychosomatic.' That is a commonplace. But he, Dr Wuchs, was the first to make the point that these gross conditions must be preceded by minute yet perfectly ascertainable reactions on the molecular level to the changing conditions of the psyche from day to day. Just as the psyche, in turn, must be affected immediately by the – er – *Empfänglichkeit* – elasticity – yes? – and receptivity of the cells.

It all sounds both miserably obvious and miserably implausible when I put it down. It sounds no less miserable when he discourses directly to me, leaning forward from his armchair in my little sitting room, his bag on the floor beside him. I want him to tell me frankly how he arrived at this way of making a living. He began as a doctor, all right; that I know; I've seen his medical diplomas hanging in frames of twisted gilt and black lacquer on the walls of his consulting rooms down in the city. As a medical student I imagine him to have been ambitious, unscrupulous, and naturally endowed with a vein of cheap fantasy. I picture him reading paperbound booklets on subjects like evolution, or the interpretation of dreams, or how to make a fortune on the stock exchange, or how to increase your vocabulary by setting aside only five minutes a day. He must have been exceptionally hungry for power; attracted to elegant surroundings and expensive objects; fascinated by the arcane and occult.

These are qualities which I have reason greatly to respect. But when I do ask him questions about his earlier years I hear nothing of them. Instead, I am told only of a lonely, disinterested search for the truth, and of a passionate concern for the betterment of the condition of man. I hear of years of patient research spent in laboratories, of papers presented to initially sceptical but subsequently converted audiences of savants in Uppsala and Paris. He tells me of intuitions he had that were later confirmed by workers in fields distant from his own, of grateful letters from people he has aided.

Yet for all his absurd boastfulness, there is something impressive about the man: I have to admit it. Most impressive of all, perhaps, is the fact that though by his own admission (or boast?) he is already in his seventy-fifth year, his stride is still so brisk, his gaze so clear, his hand so steady, his voice so firm, he orders his thoughts with so little difficulty. No question but that he is a fine advertisement for his own brands of medicine. He wears light-brown linen suits, and fancy shoes in tan and white; his cuff-links are of gold and have his initials engraved chastely upon them; the soap he uses might have been expressly manufactured for medical men, being both sweet and astringent to the nostrils. I positively enjoy having those large, perfumed hands of his busy themselves about me, when he takes my pulse, pulls down my lower eyelid to peer into my eyeball (not a job I would enjoy), listens to my lungs and heartbeat through his stethoscope, or ties around my arm the apparatus that measures my blood pressure. There are also various less orthodox gauges which he brings with him from time to time, and which are supposed to measure everything from the strength of my grip to the *Empfänglichkeit* of my sphincter . . .

He is most punctilious about his examinations. I grant him that, too. Then I lower my trousers, lie down with my eyes closed, and wait with all my senses at the ready for the reek of disinfectant, the cold touch of the cotton wool that carries it to my skin, the clinking of his little bottles, the faint, fierce jab of the needle in my hip.

So the days go by. In the evenings I sit here at my desk, like someone in a trance and get on with the job I've given myself.

I haven't said a word to Dr Wuchs about my work: about this attack of graphomania I've been the victim of ever since arriving here. I don't intend telling him about it. It's my secret. It does no harm. (I believe.) It keeps me busy. If I want to fill with words like these page upon page of the elegant, whisper-thin stationery provided by the management, why shouldn't I?

My hand moves, I watch the line it makes stretch across the page, I begin again. Each line, as it appears, makes me wonder what its successor will be. Then I find out. Then I'm filled with a renewed curiosity about the next. I can't imagine anything more likely to kill that simple pleasure than to have old Wuchs fixing his ponderous gaze on the results, *ja, ja,* and asking me, *zum Beispiel,* what I think Gerhard and Susie and Maureen represent in my subconscious

35

mind. (If I knew, you fool, they probably wouldn't be there!) Not to speak of Timothy himself, my contemporary, who pretends to be what he isn't.

Writing one's memoirs – it's a traditional occupation for hotel rooms, after all.

And if they're not mine? Should I really find that so surprising? I wouldn't be here, I remind myself, if I didn't need to be here. This morning I was walking through the woods, along a bone-dry path, with no water even in the rutted drainage channel alongside it. All of a sudden I see a frog on the ground directly in front of me. Its eyes protrude from the top of its head, its fingers arch in a tiny grip on the surface of the path, there's a pulse working away inside its yellow, wrinkled armpit, its plump hindquarters are spread like those of a woman at certain moments of intricate pleasure. I even have time to wonder, as I approach it, how it can bear to let its mucous-soft belly rest on the dirt, and why it doesn't leap away from my footfall (with an inward tension of my own, anticipating that jump) – when the frog turns into a leaf. An ordinary, motionless leaf, blown there long before.

Anybody could make such a mistake? Perhaps. But the vividness of it! The completeness! The way my heart started to pound when I realised how I'd been deceived! Or deceived myself, rather. The sense of having been there – here – so many times before . . .

Come to think of it, at every moment I half-expect to startle Timothy into a leap away from me, out of sight; then I find him to be nothing more than a leaf, too. A sheet of paper. With my lines scrawled across it.

Well, I've done my bit for today. It's time for bed.

36

More than time. A car passes at a distance, going downhill. Some footsteps crunch on the gravelled terrace, two storeys below my window. The rest of the hotel murmurs discreetly, slams a door, blows a nose. The trees outside are no more than an irregular rim of shadow, cupping the lights of the city in the valley far below. The lights flicker softly, they wink at me with a sly, Swiss complicity. I feel as though I could lean out of the window and blow them out with a single breath.

Delusions of grandeur, too –!

In the wake of a German bomber, Maureen Sullivan had been pulled out of the rubble of the Bloomsbury hotel in which she had been working. Physically she was unharmed. But she had never been the same again 'in the mind'. That was what she told Timothy. She pointed to both sides of her head, to show him where the damage had been done. Her forefingers were aimed just above her light, vacant, pale-brown eyes. If any unexpected demand was made of her, they would at once be filled with panic; some time always had to pass before the vacancy and brightness of her gaze would be restored.

When Timothy asked her what she had been like before the bombing, she answered, 'Lively, by Jesus!'

Her teeth were large and crooked; her hair, which

had been golden when she had come from Ireland, had depreciated to the colour of a baser, coppery alloy, and hung in strands to her shoulders. She walked with her thighs kept closely together, taking strides much too short for the length of her thick, dull legs. Though fashions changed, her skirts always hung just below her knees, to which they clung with a feeble, flapping persistence.

These were the charms with which she had attracted the attention of Gerhard Fogel. He had come into Robinsons to buy his cigarettes one day. The panic in her eyes when she had to work out his change gave him a sense of security. The chafing of her knees when he passed her in the high street the next day reminded him vaguely of appetites he had left behind in Germany, several years before.

He too can be charitably described as a victim of the war. Of Hitler, anyway. He had once been a student of architecture. Then he had had to abandon his studies and run from Germany. The other members of his family – father, mother, sister – were supposed to follow him. The war broke out before they managed to get away, and he never heard of them again. Instead, he read about them in newspapers. He saw photographs of them, or of what might have been them, in newsreels. Later there were books written about them. Some of the books, in lurid covers, were sold in specialised bookshops along with other articles in dubious taste. By that time Gerhard Fogel had lost his curiosity about the world. He no longer nourished ambitions to become an architect. He no longer had ambitions.

His courtship of Maureen Sullivan was brief, and

was conducted for the most part in silence on both sides. Once they went to the cinema. Once they went to Alexandra Palace, where they sat on the grass and looked at the Wood Green gasometers and the railway lines from Kings Cross. Several times they walked up and down the high street, pausing to study shop windows and advertisement signs. Originally Maureen had been brought to Hornsey by a porter in the hospital to which she'd been sent after the bombing; he had found a room and a job for her, and had visited her as often as his wife's negligence allowed him to. Then he ceased to come. Gerhard, recently discharged from the Pioneer Corps, was living in a room not far from hers. He had started working as a draughtsman in the borough council's engineering department.

It was towards the end of the war. Food was rationed. Coal was rationed. Many bombed-out buildings gaped in astonishment at others even more ruined than themselves. The nights were like caverns. Comforts of any kind were hard to come by. Accordingly, the half-man proposed to the half-wit, and was accepted on the turn.

'I always liked a quiet sort of a man. For company,' Maureen explained to Timothy.

'And Mr Truter?' Timothy asked, excited and deliciously tormented by his own jealousy. 'Is he quiet too?'

Maureen reflected before answering. 'Sometimes he can be a little wild, for such a respectable man.'

She had been back twice to her home in Ireland during the years she had been living in London: once to attend her mother's funeral and once to attend her

41

father's. She came back from these expeditions with photographs which she would sometimes, as a special treat, show to Timothy. On each there appeared a coffin, a group of men in double-breasted black suits around it, and a priest with the proud but demanding air of a football coach alongside his team.

Gerhard had never gone back to Germany. Shortly after his marriage he resigned from the borough council and set himself up as a painter. An artist. Not of an exalted kind. He turned the back bedroom of the little house they had rented into his studio. It soon became the usual mess of brushes thrust into bottles, canvases stacked against one another in corners, and tubes of paint lying about in various stages of detumescence. He was a journeyman painter, so to speak. He had printed cards pinned up in the noticeboards outside tobacconists and newsagents: *Portraits Painted, Photographs Coloured, Old Paintings Restored, Landscapes, Seascapes, Still Lifes on Request, Signwriting of Artistic Quality*, with his name and address underneath. Before he learned (more or less at the time of puberty) to be ashamed of these cards, Timothy was very proud of them. It seemed to him a great distinction to have a father whose name was stuck up outside shops, with his address underneath and a list of his skills above. In addition, Gerhard had connections with various small firms of builders and interior decorators, and did murals for them. For Spanish restaurants, Spanish dancers. For restaurants owned by Greeks, the Parthenon under a luridly blue sky.

A version of pastoral: to have been the only son, born belatedly, to a couple who lived at peace among the tilted terraces of north London. A suitable location for Gerhard and Maureen Fogel. For Timothy. For white-cuffed, round-faced, obliging Mr Truter, who was so light of tread for a man so plump, and who went industriously about his business from house to house, his brief-case always tucked into his armpit. For Miss Green, known to a few daring spirits as Polly, the teacher with a long, hooked nose, who stank of strong tea and whose middle finger was clothed in a sinister black fingerstall. (It was rumoured that in a fit of anger she had driven the point of a lead pencil under her nail; that the lead had broken off; that it would remain there forever.) For Mr Brooks, another teacher much adored by our hero, in spite of his froggy, quivering throat and the uplifted but never-used rubber strap which he referred to in ominous third-person form as 'my fine old friend, Mr Dunlop'.

Above them all, the few whose names and faces were known and the many who were strangers, were chimney-pots ranged in rows like the spines on a dragon's back, and a sky never emptied of its vapours. Around them, coil upon coil of brick and slate. To navigate by, through yellow mornings of fog and dazzlingly black and silver evenings of rain, a mother's large, firm hand, enclosing his.

She always brought him safely home, to the only house in which it was possible for him to live, among all the others that looked so much like his from the outside and were so unimaginable within. The house itself seemed to remember that it was his, and made him welcome every time he returned to it. Some places inside it, however, were more grudging than others in their welcome, especially when the light began to fail at the end of every day. The kitchen was always a safe and cheerful place to be in, it was always glad to have him; the little front hall, on the other hand, contained more than a hint of menace, which not even his mother's presence could entirely abolish. In the kitchen there was warmth and activity: pots on the gas stove, peelings and tea leaves in the rubbish bin, steam on the windows insulating the room from the darkness beyond. In the hall, the narrow staircase silently debouched strange reflections of itself on to a floor of polished linoleum; the hallstand leaned back against the wall with a trapped, desperate air, and held before it the only weapons it had, its prongs for coats to hang on. From the ceiling, much the tallest in the house, there hung a lightshade that was as copiously befringed as a lady in an eastern tale, and that looked quite capable of lowering itself and advancing in stately fashion on a boy whose back was turned.

Outside, the rear garden was marked off by brick walls whose crumbling mortar and inexplicable bulges made them look immensely old to Timothy, older than the house itself. He didn't feel the garden to be as good or safe a place for him as the grown-ups seemed to think it was, if only because of the peculiar behaviour of a row of poplar trees planted against the back fence. Disproportionately large for the size of the garden, they were always waving their branches and shivering their leaves, as if threatening Timothy and trembling in fear of him simultaneously. He disliked both suggestions. He much preferred to sit in the tiny front porch of the house, where he could watch whoever went by on the pavement without being noticed himself. He liked the street's subtle low cambers and lines, the kerb raised its necessary few inches above the gutter, and the blocks along the pavement lying head to head, foot to foot, side to side, each imprisoning the others forever, in an infinite turn and turn about. There was also a manhole cover in the middle of the street he was especially fond of: it had such a round face and body all in one, he was sure it was good natured, it would do him no harm.

There were many other places he liked. His mother's bed. The sweet shop his mother used to work in, in that indescribably remote period before he was born. The shoe shop where, out of shiny white cardboard boxes and rustling wrappings of tissue paper (each of these with its own distinctive, lesser smell) there emerged shoes of such an odorous matching brilliance he could hardly breathe in their presence. The station which his father sometimes took him to, instead of to the park, and which he liked most for its air of regretfulness just after a train had left.

How strange it was that these places filled him with cravings, instead of setting him at peace. When he thought of them he craved to see them again; when he saw them, he craved for he knew not what. Sometimes he actually cried with longing at the sight of them: especially of empty Omdurman Terrace on a sunny afternoon, when he sat by himself looking out at it from his hidden point of observation. It seemed to be waiting for what he couldn't really believe would ever come: perhaps for the day when there would at last be nobody, neither Timothy nor anyone else, to look at it. Then he too would inexplicably long for that day, his eyes filled with sweet tears at the thought. He felt much the same on his visits with his parents to Alexandra Palace, when he stood high above the northern reaches of London and saw roof-tops, streets, and open spaces rammed irregularly together, as if all upon one plane, like a rough, veined rock of great size and no shape, lying at a tilt where time had left it. It looked like a phenomenon of nature, as adventitious as any other, having nothing to do with the plans and directions of men. For that very reason he and everybody else who lived in its crevices and humps seemed to him to be intruders. All of them. One day they would have to go.

What he liked could make him cry. What he didn't like – the darkly perverted taste of marmalade, say, or the sound of his father's voice raised angrily against him or his mother – made him feel that he would never be able to cry again. Susie Sendin, whom he liked best in the world made him do both, first the one and then the other, over and over again.

No post since coming here. No phone calls either. I must remember to ask at the desk if there's been anything for me. So far I've hardly exchanged a word with the creature in blue worsted and gold piping who usually sits there. He looks as if he would cheerfully let you roll about the floor in agony before him, unless you happened to 'catch his eye' in the course of your writhings. Then he would at once be all solicitude.

How strange – now I've written it, I realise I might have seen the very end of an incident rather like that when I first arrived. Raised voices were suddenly hushed, a man was being led away forcibly down the corridor, a carpet was rucked up in one corner. Or so it appeared to me, fleetingly. A little out of breath, people were straightening their jackets and re-adjusting their cuffs. But the youngster at the desk sat undisturbed in front of his numbered pigeon-holes and dangling bunches of keys. That's what he had been paid to do, so that's what he did.

On second thoughts, I won't bother to approach him. It's probably wiser not to. I'll hear soon enough if people really do want to get hold of me. If nobody tries to, so much the better. I didn't come here to worry about what I left behind. It all seems so remote. I'm sure everyone is managing perfectly well without me.

It's my new 'friends', Timothy and the rest of them, who need me now if they are to get anywhere at all. Generously, I offer them my cooperation; even more generously, I refrain from asking them what exactly they are up to.

When Timothy went back in his mind to that memory of a park, a swing, a fall from which all his other memories seemed to extend in an unbroken chain towards him, there came into its aboriginal, time-darkened silence a single word. A name. Susie. Susie. Susie.

He could never admit to himself that the Susie in the park might not have been the girl who was now in his class at school. He would as soon have believed that elsewhere in the world there could be found another girl with exactly the face and character of the Susie he knew. Or that his Susie could look like Myrtle Collins from two doors up the road, and smell of toast and liniment like her. Or, for that matter, that she could be a boy like freckled, sand-coloured Eddie

Antrobus, who was so fat he had titties that shook like a grown-up lady's when he ran. Such things were evidently impossible, self-contradictory.

Susie Sendin had only one existence; it was entwined with his. She had only one set of attributes; he knew them all. They were his possessions, indeed, as well as hers, if only because he was able to count them over repeatedly.

For instance, there were a few pale freckles, just a few, quite unlike Eddie's plethora, under Susie's eyes; they rested in a safe hollow over her cheekbones. He knew all about those freckles; even why those under one eye had to be a shade darker than those under the other. To please him, of course! When Susie put her head back her hair hung farther back yet, away from her neck, in a soft, shining, light brown collapse that he wanted to gather with his open fingers, precisely in order to feel it run away again. He knew, with an anticipation so keen it was like a memory, just how light her hair would be in his hand, and also how heavy. Her lower teeth were so crooked and crowded that even when her lips were closed he could still make out the irregular line behind them; again, he knew every secret word, addressed to him only, of which that line was composed. Sometimes her eyes looked green, sometimes brown, but always they had tiny, triangular flecks or chips of a darker colour like stone embedded in them. He did not know what difference those flint-like chips made to her sight, in their wonderful circular setting of varying gleam and hue. But he did know the difference they made to him. He wanted to impress her so much that they would fall with a little click of astonishment or terror out of her eyes and into a silk-lined box he would have ready for them. He would immediately put a jewelled lid on the box, to make sure that they would never get lost. Then he would lead poor blind Susie about, wherever she wanted to go.

No, wherever he wanted to go.

In the meantime he followed her. Even in his schoolwork. She was good at hers, and it was because he wanted to make her take notice of him that he finally decided to master the letters and numbers in his books. During playtimes, when his voice blended so loudly with the cries of all the other children that their common din ascended to the ears of Gerhard Fogel, making him pause from his work in his studio and perhaps go vaguely downstairs to put a kettle on the gas stove for his tea – during these playtimes Timothy watched out for Susie, and played as near to her as he could, always hoping that she would be drawn into his games, or he into hers.

He had often said to his mother that Susie was his 'best friend' at school. But it wasn't true; he just wanted it to be true. He had also often told her that he wanted Susie to come to his house to play with him. 'Why don't you ask her?' Maureen suggested, reasonably enough. Timothy was silent each time. He had simply never dared to do it.

One day, however, without preparation, speaking out of the heat and breathlessness of a playtime that had just ended, as they ran with others through the lobby on their way back to their classroom, he did ask Susie to come to his house to play. She turned her flushed face to him.

'I'll have to ask my mum.'

Behind them the swing doors of the lobby passed one another with a flabby, double slap of the air. But his heart held still. He was no longer running. Susie had gone in front of him and was looking back.

'Ask her, then.'

'All right.'

The bell that marked the end of playtime had not yet stopped ringing. He heard it with astonishment. So quick! So easy! She ran ahead. Other children ran. The world ran, it streamed beneath him, and he walked on it or through it without stumbling.

When he came home he told his mother that Susie was coming to play with him soon. He spoke as casually as he could, feeling it to be safer not to display too much emotion. Presently, while she was sitting at the kitchen table and drinking her afternoon tea, he came and cuddled up close to her. That also was done for safety's sake, though he did not know what he feared. She bent over him, put the point of her chin on the top of his head, and pressed down. It was a way she had: a hard, fond, animal caress. He always liked it when she did it to him. Perhaps most of all he liked the sound that his hair made as it was squashed flat against his skull. He remained in her arms until Maureen, whose eyes had been browsing vacantly on the stained, beige-coloured wall of the kitchen, was disturbed by an agitation of bird voices outside the window, like the blades of many scissors rapidly opening and closing. 'Come, Timmy,' she said, 'let's go into the garden and give the birdies some crumbs, and see how they swallow them up.'

But the birds fled when they opened the kitchen door. After the confinement of the room, all space outside seemed to be awhirl, intoxicated, under the evening's canopy of stillness. Dark-green light welled up stanchlessly from the lawn; now here, now there, dark blue light flapped among the leaves of the poplar trees, but could not get away. Timothy hopped about the lawn, pretending to be a bird, and Maureen fed him pretend crumbs which he pretended to gobble up.

The next morning Susie told him that her mummy had said she could not come and play at his house.

'Why not?'

'My mummy says that everyone knows about your mummy and Mr Truter.'

Heat flared up at the back of his naked knees. He felt the strength of his legs burn away beneath him where he stood, in front of the work-table Susie shared with another girl. The freckles below her eyes were suddenly as pitiless as a constellation of stars determining his fate. She bent her head, eclipsing them, in order to get on with the crayon drawing she had been busy with. Around them was the never-ceasing hum and scrape and squeak of the classroom. Heads bobbed closer to one another or parted, rose, turned, came together again. Timothy was unable to move. Susie's crayon went back and forth. With every line, more and more of the basin-shaped lake she was drawing filled up from below with blue, blue water. A boat complete with stiff, triangular sails hung in mid-air, waiting for the level of the water to reach its keel. Then it would sail away.

He did not see it go. Somehow he managed to drag

himself back to his desk. Once he was seated, the flame left his enfeebled legs, and scorched the back of his neck instead. In his chest there was a stifling sense of apprehension, as though some dreadful event was about to befall him. It was no comfort to him to think that it had already happened. Again and again tears reduced the classroom to a flat silver shimmer of light, with all the colours of the rainbow around its edges. Furtively he wiped or blinked the blur away. The school day went on. He looked at books and pictures, he stared at Mr Brooks, he wrote, he went into the playground and spent as much of the break as he dared to in the noisome, trickling coolness of the lavatory. The bell rang again and he returned to his chair. He pretended to laugh when the others laughed. He wanted to be hidden among them, unnoticeable; to pretend to them and to himself that he was as innocent as he had been when he had set out for school in the morning, as ignorant of his own shame and his mother's guilt. He listened to the slow babble of little Tommy Hewitt, his partner at the table, of whom he had never before been afraid, but whose pale, red-nosed face he now surreptitiously studied for signs of a knowingness that had not previously been there. When Tommy left the table he felt exposed and abandoned; when Tommy returned to it he was afraid of what he might have learned while he had been away. Then Tommy went away again, and Susie slipped into his place. Timothy began to tremble. The heat flared up and crept round his neck to cover his face.

'What does your mummy do with Mr Truter?'

He trembled. He did not answer.

54

'Why don't you tell me?'

Trembling, he shook his head.

'You must know,' she hissed. 'You've got to tell me.'

He tried vainly to swallow his own dryness, but did not speak. She put her head down and looked up at him from below. He could not escape from her gaze. Her mouth was open, revealing crooked teeth and a gleaming spider's thread of saliva.

'I think,' she said slowly. 'that your mummy does pooffy-poof with Mr Truter.'

He could not speak. Nor could he stop trembling. Finally he nodded, afraid that a denial might lead to even more sinister and more mysterious accusations.

'She does pooffy-poof with your daddy, too.'

Again he nodded.

She slipped away. He remained alone. First his mother had betrayed him with the acts that Susie had named but not explained; now he had betrayed her with his nods. He was doubly alone. Beyond all help. Susie's head was somewhere among all the other dark and fair heads in the classroom. She just had to open her mouth and everyone in the room would learn why he was unfit to be played with. They would know even better than he did, for he was sure that unlike himself they would all know the meaning of the word that Susie had uttered. Even if she didn't say it again today, it would still be there, within her mouth, ready to be made public at any time.

When Timothy got home he wandered out alone into the back garden. He had said to his mother that he did not want any tea; that was all he had said since meeting her at the school gates. It had been unthinkable for him to tell her what had happened. He knew he would be unable to tell anyone about it as long as he lived. Simply to be on his own in the garden was a great relief to him; at the same time he despaired because he wouldn't be able to remain alone for the rest of his life.

Most of the garden was in shadow. The sun shone only on the tops of the poplar trees. For once their leaves were still. Under the branches it was always cooler than elsewhere, and there was a smell of mould in the air: an ancient, reticent odour, belonging exclusively to corners and shade. Out of the soil immediately next to the wall there protruded some builders' shards that unknown men had once buried and time had since exposed. The surface of the bricks in the wall had been eaten away by London smoke and acid over the years, and as a result they were curiously porous, almost sponge-like in appearance. They looked black and brown only from a distance; when you came closer you saw them to be mauve and yellow as well. Lichen grew in the long horizontal and brief upright lines of mortar that kept them together.

Timothy leaned his forehead against the wall. He closed his eyes. He wanted to do away completely with his recollection of the day. To have no shred of it left in his consciousness. To have no consciousness.

He succeeded. He became brick.

No, no comments, no criticisms, no head-shakings, no expostulations, nothing. It's not my job. Not my responsibility.

Still – poor little devil!

Timothy became brick. He became iron. He became stone. He became wood. He became leather. He became china. He became glass.

He had learned the knack. It was easy, once he had discovered that it could be done. He took whatever substance he wanted to turn himself into, he put it against his forehead, he closed his eyes, and he waited.

At first he had to be alone. Later, when he became more skilled, he found that he could undergo such transmutations even in the company of others. Provided he could shut their presence out of his consciousness for long enough.

For how long? He did not know. How long did he remain possessed by the substance he had become, or possessing it? He did not know that either. The questions made no sense. Time belonged to life and movement. Outside them, time did not exist. How could it? It was left behind, he was divested of it, as he was divested of every other principle or condition of his own individuality.

He became paper. He became brass. He became bone. He became slate. He became soap. He became sugar. He became coal.

He experimented eagerly, but not always successfully. There were some substances that always remained beyond him, starkly impenetrable or unwearyingly evasive – liquids, living matter (even of the vegetable kind), man-made plastics and fibres, gas. Each time, he wearied before they did. He could not become the obscure accumulations of stuff – soapy, sticky, and hairy all at once – that were to be found in crevices behind the bent, pug-like legs of their old bathtub. He could not become a part of any machine in motion, or of radio and television sets even when they were switched off. He could not become anything that had once belonged to his own body: hair, fingernails, faeces. He was more successful with waste from the bodies of others, though he never much enjoyed those particular operations.

He became his father's paint. He became the milk of magnesia tablets which his mother took for her occasional bouts of indigestion. He became sweets, chalk, string, potato crisps, tobacco ash, bread. Compound substances presented no more difficulty to him than simple ones. He could even transform himself into articles composed of more than one substance which were merely bonded together. He became books, hairbrushes, shoes, knives with bone handles, pencils.

He didn't tell anyone about his new-found powers. He was afraid he might lose them if he spoke about them. He was also afraid that people would laugh at him. Yet he believed that there was nothing singular about him. Everyone could do what he was able to do. Indeed, everyone did. They had all found this release from pain and desire, from the passage of time which brought your world to you and in the same mysterious movement took it relentlessly from you. Without such a faculty men and women wouldn't have been able to carry on for so long. They would never have been able to bear their individual sentience, their severance from the materials of which they were composed.

These were not his words at the time. But they were his beliefs nevertheless.

He became sponge, porcelain, lead, bacon-rind, money, cotton wool, mother-of-pearl, glazed tiles, quarry tiles and roofing tiles.

He learned that no more from within than without was matter undifferentiated. He knew and was known by gravity and buoyancy, hardness and malleability, friability and cohesion, fibrousness and flocculence, translucence and opacity. Metal tingled within him; rubber winced; wood cramped itself around its own knots; glass dreamed it wasn't there; cold stone ridges and flutings shouldered the world of air aside; fibres of hessian laced themselves over and under each other like lovers. The gates of matter opened for him. He was taken into garden after garden of eternal rigidity and symmetry, whose repose he did not disturb, for with his entry their repose became his own.

It was never difficult for him to resume his identity once again. As with being conceived or born, he had no choice in the matter. It just happened. His self-hood returned to him. It brimmed up rapidly and silently within him, while his other existence contracted and vanished in its own dimension. He heard again his mother's soft, insistent call of 'Timmee, Timmee' (to his ears it always sounded like a call of another kind – 'To *me!* To *me!*); he became aware of his father's earnest, clerkly presence, and heard him breathing whistlingly through his nose; he felt Tommy Hewitt wriggling on the seat beside him; he saw Mr Brooks's absurd, ranine gaze fixed upon him and heard the unleashed Mr Dunlop whistling past his ears. There were times, too, when he came to himself to the chant of 'Pooffy-poof Timothy' from a group of children organised and urged on by Susie Sendin. More than once she put up her little brother, Laurence, who was much smaller than Timothy, much swarthier, and much fiercer, to challenge him to a fight; when he declined the challenge she and Laurence pursued him across the playground yelling, 'Cowardy, cowardy custard'.

He did not try to avoid her (except when he was in full flight from her), nor did he smile in sickly appeal and proffer bribes of sweets and pennies to her. Instead, he was withdrawn and dreamy, he looked at her from his pallid, wide-spaced eyes as indifferently as at everyone else in the classroom. It maddened her. She did not know that in morning assembly he repeatedly tried to become the material of her dress, of which he held a thin scrap between his fingers, away from her breathing, moving hips. He never succeeded. Once, however, he crept back into the classroom after school in defiance of the regulations, and managed to transform himself into the wood and metal of her desk. He remained there, within it, inseparable from it, until the cleaning women disturbed him.

By that time all the mums had gone from the school gates, except for patient Maureen. She hadn't dared to come into the school grounds to look for him. Now she ran forward with many chafing sounds from her garments.

'Timmy, where have you been? Why are you so late?'

'I can't remember, mummy.'

Maureen and Gerhard consulted together. As a result, Maureen bought a bottle of malt and cod liver oil, from which she fed Timothy a spoonful after supper every evening. He did not object. He liked the taste and texture of the stuff. He liked even more the distinctive brown glass of the barrel-shaped bottle in which the malt came, and duly transformed himself into it at the earliest opportunity.

Eventually Gerhard went to speak to Mr Brooks about Timothy's 'dreaminess', as his parents called it. 'It's a phase,' Mr Brooks answered confidently. 'Many children go through it at this stage. I'm sure you did in your time – ha-ha!' Gerhard looked doubtful, and Mr Brooks felt that possibly he had gone too far, especially as Gerhard still looked like a pretty dreamy character to him. 'Anyway, I did. I remember it well. Just see that there's plenty for him to do at home, and I'm sure he'll be all right.'

Gerhard went home with this message. He found Timothy sitting on the bench against the inside wall of the little porch. The back of his head rested against a stucco rosette plastered on to the brickwork. Was he an *Epileptiker*? The word came from nowhere into Gerhard's mind. He put his hand on the boy's shoulder. Timothy opened his eyes at once.

'Hullo, papa.'

'Hullo, Timothy. Why do you sit here – in this fashion – ? Do you feel quite well?'

A smile. A smile of satisfaction. Not a smile to set a father's heart at rest. Least of all a father who has always had reason to hope or fear that his son may have been marked out for a special destiny.

So they took Timothy to see the doctor: a man whose teeth were so white and whose features were so distinctly outlined that even from the other end of the room his patients had the impression they were looking at him in close-up. When he bent over them, their senses swam. He gave Timothy a chocolate which he took from a drawer in his desk, breathed upon the coin-like end of his stethescope to warm it up, and then proceeded with his examination. When he had finished he recommended that Maureen should continue with the malt and cod liver oil she was giving Timothy, and should begin at once with the iron tablets for which he wrote out a prescription.

Timothy took the iron tablets. He became the iron tablets. Then Timothy turned himself into the veneered plywood wardrobe in Gerhard and Maureen's bedroom. He heard nothing; he saw nothing; he was rammed flat, dried out, laminated; he had no weight but to sustain his own surfaces, back and front; he was sealed everywhere in gleaming varnish, except for a few splintered or corrugated patches. He could have remained thus forever, wholly a part of it, part of its wholeness, if it had not been for his mother's voice.

She summoned him back into his single self. 'To me!' she called. 'Come to *me*!'

He went to her. He was sundered from what he had been. He burst through the door of the wardrobe. The bed boiled and heaved. Hairy limbs flew across the room, and resolved themselves into a man holding a pair of charcoal grey trousers in front of him. His mother's flesh rose towards Timothy like a tidal wave. It broke directly over his head. 'I'll have your life!' she yelled in the pure, thick accents of county Kerry. He was banged on the back and on the side of the head, he was knocked upside down, he was thrown into a corner of the wardrobe like a bundle of dirty linen.

But it wasn't he who burst into tears; it was his mother.

Later there were recriminations between Gerhard and Maureen. Hadn't she told him that Myrtle Collins's mother was looking after Timothy that afternoon? If not, who had told him so? Timothy himself? Gerhard could not remember. Nor could she. They stared at Timothy, who was playing quietly and self-consciously on the sitting room floor. Most of the floor was covered by a worn, checked Wilton carpet, with which Timothy was better acquainted than either of his parents could have guessed. Around the edges of the carpet were floorboards stained black; they too had been substance of his substance, wood of his wood. He drove a toy car along one row of checks, and looked to the left and right, as he had so often been told to do when out walking in the streets with his mother, before turning the car to proceed along another row.

He rose when Maureen told him it was time to go to bed. He went upstairs, washed his face, cleaned his teeth, put on his pyjamas and got into bed. Even after the thorough washing he had just given his face, he could still feel his mother's smack across his temple. He could also feel the blow of her fist in the small of his back. These places were not sore. On the contrary, they felt warm and rich; they were a source of comfort to him; it was as if they already knew all that the rest of him need no longer be anxious to learn. Maureen's goodnight kiss, before she closed his bedroom door, faded and was gone almost immediately. She kissed him every night. But she had never hit him before.

Once she was out of the room, he became the coir of his mattress, the feathers in his pillow, the ticking in which both were covered, the metal frame of his bed, the wooden legs bolted on to it, the wool of his blankets, the cotton of his sheets, the wax of his crayons, the canvas of the picture his father had painted for him of a steam engine pulling out of a station, the painted steam engine itself, a handful of soot which he scraped out of the chimney above his never-used fireplace. He woke from each of these states without knowing what had brought him out of it and fell into the next without knowing he was about to do so. He couldn't stop himself. He was afraid to try, lest he should miss some experience more illuminating than any that had gone before. The first few birds were already making their noises outside, like those of fingers carefully ringing and rubbing the dawn-tinted bowl of the sky, before he finally managed to fall asleep.

The next day was Saturday. In honour of the weekend Gerhard abandoned the paint-smeared linen coat and baggy jersey (knitted to an unvarying pattern by Maureen, though in different colours from year to year) which he usually wore, and put on a smart sports jacket, a newly laundered shirt, and a polka-dotted bow tie. It was in this outfit that he took his son for a walk to the park. On the way back, with many pauses, frowns, and earnest cranings forward of his head, he made his position clear to himself, at least, if not to Timothy.

It was all a lot of nonsense! So much fuss over such a little thing! A childish business! 'Huggy, cuddly, snuggly – putting handy-pandies into this place and that . . . Where they don't usually go. Babies want to play like that, and children. And when we're grown up, then we also have to do it sometimes . . . . Believe me, one day when you're older you'll remember what I tell you, and then you'll understand my meanings . . . ' He hadn't suggested that Mr Truter should come once a week, regular. Nor had Timothy's mother. It had been Mr Truter's idea right from the start. A married man, too, which was a remarkable thing . . . And it wasn't as though it was so easy to make a good living nowadays, not at all. But enough was enough. Timothy wasn't to worry. There was no need for him to hide in wardrobes. Nothing for him to grow dreamy about. Anyone could see that he was getting to be a big boy. He, Gerhard, expected great things from Timothy. He always had. He didn't yet know what they would be. Who could tell?

Just above the Highgate Hill an engorged red sun gazed down upon them. Unswervingly, through streets enfolded within streets for tens of miles in every direction, they made their way towards the sketchy Saturday evening meal prepared for them by Maureen. They walked hand in hand, and in silence, once Gerhard had concluded his statement. Timothy offered no confidences in return. Nor did he comment on what he had been told. Gerhard apparently did not expect him to.

Gerhard's weekend treats included not only a change of clothing, but also, in the evenings, small Dutch cigars and modest amounts of brandy and water. Timothy's treat was to be allowed to stay up later than usual to look at the rainy, grainy pictures on the television set they had bought second-hand from a shop up the road. Maureen's was to go on her weekly visit to her friend Mrs Robinson, the wife of her former employer.

That Saturday evening she came back with the news that Mrs Robinson had heard that Mrs Davis of The Sewing Basket was looking for someone to help her. Part-time. Just what she wanted.

It was a peaceful evening. Timothy tried to turn himself into shadow; then into lamplight. He failed both times. He wondered what it would be like to be wind, words, a cloud, a star, a note of music, not his eye or his mother's but the glance between them.

The chamber maid loves to talk. She talks even while she's holding a sheet or towel under her chin, in the manner of all bed-making women, so that she'll have her hands free to fold it up. When she bends over to tuck in a blanket or empty my waste paper basket, her skirt climbs high up the back of her bare legs, revealing most of her thighs and the crack of shadow between them. Which I like of course, remotely. Her favourite subject of conversation is how expensive everything is nowadays. I suspect it's less a complaint on her part, or even a plea for a large tip, than a way of trying to make me feel guilty for being able to stay here. She also speaks to me about her young man, who apparently works up at the swimming bath. I think she would like me to understand that he is one of the gleaming, cotton-trousered fellows with sun-bleached hair who stand about the pool all day, in attitudes pleasing both to themselves and to all onlookers. But perhaps he does nothing more than sweep out the cubicles.

Downstairs I make conversation once again with Marnie. She's American. In her mid-thirties. Not really my age bracket, but nearer to it than anyone else in this place. Her husband is a big man in a super-market chain. Or something like that. She has two sons who are spending the summer with her mother in New Jersey. Or somewhere like that. She has a dis-tinctive smell. Even in the lounge, despite all the other odours in the air – cigarette smoke, gin, tea, the leaden smell of upholstery and carpeting – I noticed it at once. The smell of her anxiety? Perhaps. Dry, faint-ly singed, sad . . . But it's impossible to describe any smell, least of all that which comes off the skin or hair of a woman with whom one is engaging in social chat. She uses little make-up. Her teeth are elaborately engineered. Above the loose, silken floral print she is wearing, her neck shows a strain which doesn't come from her age alone. The same strain is in her voice, and in the single upright line between her plucked and pencilled eyebrows.

So then, how are you this morning, and won't you have some more coffee, and when is your husband joining you, and how old are your sons, and of course I'd love to see their photographs, and what charming boys they are – so lively! – and –

Her eyes are her best feature: they really are more violet than blue. She wears glasses to read with. They are lying on the table next to her book and handbag.

When she looks away from me the strain of peering short-sightedly into the distance shows at once in the deepening of that line between her brows. Women and their glasses! There's a subject to drive a man distraught.

And me? How kind of her to ask. But there isn't much that I can tell her about myself. No news. I've taken a few more little walks, I'm going into town tomorrow, I think I am feeling better for the treatment I've been having while I'm here. Yes, indeed, I am under treatment, that's why I came. I was rather rundown before leaving London. Nervous fatigue, I suppose it could be called. And I was recommended to this particular place and to –

Dr Wuchs! No! What a coincidence! It appears that Marnie, too, while she waits for her husband to join her, is undergoing treatment at the hands of the doctor.

In the silence that follows we exchange a guilty, mutually speculative glance. Then we look at the people gathered in small groups across the width of the room and on the open sunlit terrace beyond, where the polished wood and cretonnes of our lounge furniture give way to glass table-tops and spidery, white ironwork. Are they all Dr Wuchs's patients? Is every seated bottom we can see punctured daily by his indefatigable needle? Every drinker of tea or coffee, every dissector of cream cake, every licker of long-handled ice cream spoon, in search of *Selbstverstehen?*

Well, we begin to talk hastily of other matters. The book she is reading. Our difficulties with the German language. The amazing charmlessness of most of the natives we have encountered. On the other hand: the cleanliness of their cities and the beauty of their countryside. The conversation lapses. She takes up her book, her spectacles, and her handbag, and sits with them on her lap for a moment; then the glasses go into the bag, which she closes with a decisive snap.

'A friend told me I should come,' she explains. 'I'm most grateful to Dr Wuchs. He's already made a great difference to how I feel about myself – and about many other things.'

'I'm glad to hear it.'

No further revelations follow. She rises, smoothing down the skirt of her dress, and goes away with the inevitable excuse of having some letters to write. She walks stiffly. Her head is craned forward a little.

If we are all patients of Dr Wuchs, two thoughts follow. Firstly, what a business the man must have! Secondly, why wasn't I told that the whole place is actually a sanatorium, and not just a hotel which happens to be comfortable for me and handy for the doctor? Why hasn't he said a word to me about the scale of his operations here? Is it just another example of his ingrained deviousness?

Which reminds me that I spoke about suicide to him yesterday afternoon. 'I have recommended it in certain cases,' he said, heavy-lidded, limp-handed, poker-faced.

'Have you ever assisted it?'

'In certain cases.' The same grave tone, the same watchful, expressionless face.

So I know more or less where I stand with him about that. (I wonder what he would charge for that small service!) Then I asked, 'And what about

72

bringing back the dead?'

He asked me to unbutton my shirt. He began to examine me. He prodded and poked, he put two fingers together and auscultated my chest, he plucked at my flesh and let it slide away between thumb and forefinger. Only then did he answer me.

'The dead come back,' he said, in a tone of curious, grim relish which I hadn't heard from him before, 'without my assistance. In their own fashion, of course. As the laws of physics and chemistry permit. And as the minds of the living allow them to, or invite them to. The more life, the more death! Nature knows no other bargains. I've learned that it's wiser not to try to outwit her.'

He put a rubber ball in my hand and asked me to clench my fist upon it as tightly as I could; the ball was attached by a piece of rubber tubing to one of his fancy gauges that stood upright on the table next to my bed. First the right hand, then the left.

'Who is it in particular that you wish to restore to life?' he asked, when he judged my attention to be sufficiently distracted.

I couldn't think of anyone. I no longer knew why I'd asked the question. I told him so, perhaps a little too abruptly.

He took the rubber ball from me and began packing his instruments away. While he was doing it he spoke about a collection of Chinese jade on view in a gallery down in the city; he himself was a collector in a small way, he told me, and had some rather fine pieces on which he would be glad to have my opinion. They were not treasures like those in the exhibition, of course; but still, my interest in such subjects being known to him – and my father such a distinguished connoisseur – he'd be flattered . . .

That would be fine. *Grossartig*. His secretary would be glad to fix up a suitable time for me. I just had to phone. And now would I please – ahm – lower a little the belt of the trousers, to expose the hip? Perhaps a little lower would be possible? Ah, thank you. He would have the injection ready in one moment, in just one moment.

No more? All silent? Gone to earth, vanished, the whole tribe of them?

It could be that they've been scared away. By what, though? I have no idea.

There hasn't been a word from them all day. I don't know how to fill in my time. I sit here sucking at the end of my pen like a bloody fool. It's extraordinary how unhappy it makes me feel to think that this whole scribbling adventure may have quietly come to its end. For no reason. Just as it began.

I was filled then, when it began, with a kind of panic. All I knew was to shout out (silently) help! intrusion! rape! where am I? etcetera. Now panic springs from the thought of being left quite on my own, to get on with being whatever I am, in this nowhere of a place, having nothing to look forward to – no developments, no surprises, no other selves to entertain.

The department store occupies an entire block of the city's main street. Its walls are of steel and black glass; they project into various prow-like corners and extremities, in an aggressive, meaningless modern fashion. Once I'm inside the building I drift down to the household equipment basement. The woman I speak to wears a simple black dress, like all the other female assistants. Just above her soft, unstable breast is a plastic badge with her name on it. Fraulein Ilse Schwabber. Not a pretty name. In English, but with a few halting phrases of German thrown in, I explain my needs, emphasising how little space there is in the apartment I have just acquired. My wife, I tell her, must feel that it is like living in a little box! *Eine kleine Büchse*! Ha-ha! Fraulein Ilse Schwabber

77

appreciates my witticism. She smiles and nods understandingly. She will do her best to help me. Yes, I am indeed from England, and it is my employers who have sent me to live in this beautiful city. We spend twenty minutes discussing makes, measurements, plumbing problems, colour schemes, the merits and demerits of enamel tops as against plastic tops. She presses leaflets on me. When I speak she appears to listen attentively; it's when she answers that I can see, by the flicker of her hazel eye within its cage of mascara, just how bored she is by what she is obliged to say. I am not offended. One could hardly expect her to be as touched as I am by my fantasies of modest domesticity in a foreign land. Finally, I indicate which range of machines and cabinets interests me the most, and tell her that I will be returning in a few days to take the matter further. *Danke schön. Bitte schön.*

From there I go to the men's clothing department, and price but do not buy some linen jackets rather like those worn by my good friend, the doctor. The weather is so much warmer here than in London, I really feel the need for lighter clothing. But the styles they offer me don't appeal. So I inspect glass and china, garden furniture, books, toys, ladies' underwear on ecstatic fibreglass torsos. The only man I see in the last-mentioned department (presumably waiting for his wife) looks fixedly at the ceiling, so that no-one will take him for a peeping tom or a fetichist. I leave him there, valiantly proving his point, and go for a ride on the moving stairs. Like an addict I respond to the lights, the acres of glass crammed with handbags and gloves, the artificially cooled gusts of air, the rows of gesticulating, talking figures repeated innumerable times, in black and white, in colour, on large screens and small, in the television department.

Then I go down the main street, looking for a cup of coffee. It's a sunny morning, but the street is not crowded. Trams clang back and forth along it. Small trees are planted at intervals on the pavement. Everything has a pleasant, unexpectedly provincial air. Under a canvas awning a man brings me a cup of coffee, a boy the pastry I ask for. After eating and drinking and staring for long enough at the men and women walking by, I get up and join them. A few blocks further on is a cobbled square, where the trams turn in their tracks with prolonged whimpers and screeches. All around are the buildings of international finance corporations. Panelled bronze doors stand above flights of marble steps; ornamentally curved iron grilles hang over narrow windows. Another hundred yards and the lake unfurls like a flag. It ripples, it snaps, it flaunts its colours in the sunshine. A park borders it on one side; along the other is a busy highway, looked down on by houses and gardens. The farthest shore is out of sight, lost somewhere between the lake's vaporous glitter and that of the sky.

The end of my day out. Back here in the limousine. Back to my desk.

Well?

I wait. I listen.

The Arizona Cafe, Crouch End Road, London N14. A weekend afternoon, during school holidays. The cafe empty but for Timothy Fogel and Laurence Sendin sitting at a yellow, plastic-topped table. The owner of the cafe bent over the racing pages of the *Evening Standard*, spread open on the counter in front of him. To his right a hissing tea-urn and a glass showcase containing ready-cut sandwiches in cerements of cellophane. A fly buzzing around the showcase in hope of getting at the sandwiches and feeding on their ham, cheese and tomato, sardine, and beef and pickle fillings.

In the end, even that fly seemed infected by the malaise of adolescence: the tedium of waiting for something to happen. It gave up throwing itself against the showcase and flew in a series of loops in the direction of the boys' table. It landed on Timothy's empty glass, which was sticky with a sediment of Coca Cola; then launched itself again to attack the glass from another angle. In mid-air, with a grab as swift as that of a chameleon's tongue, Laurence had caught the fly in his hand.

The two boys looked at each other, Laurence holding out the hand in which the captured fly buzzed.

What was he to do with it? To squash it would be disgusting. To let it go would be futile. He decided, finally, to close his hand on it. The fly died with a crack. A surprisingly loud crack for so tiny a creature. Laurence dropped its corpse into his glass, and wiped off with a dirty handkerchief what remained of its entrails on the heel of his hand.

'Fly snot,' he explained.

Not a wonderfully witty remark. But it was sufficient to set them off laughing with such smothered intensity that the owner of the cafe had to look up from his newspaper to see what the joke was all about. By that time each boy was simply laughing at the other's distorted face. Then they wiped their eyes and sat in silence again.

Laurence lit a cigarette. With audible contractions of his throat, and with lips that pouted open and closed like a fish's, he began to blow smoke rings. Around his small, swarthy face there hung two loops of hair, framing it like a pair of brackets, as if what he showed of himself was merely provisional, a temporary fascia only. Timothy looked at the smoke rings, then turned his gaze towards the street. A series of grotesquely undulating shadows in the frosted lower half of the cafe window supported the quite normal heads and shoulders of passersby. Every now and again a shadow without a head above it would waggle by; then a child would cross the lighted space of the doorway. The sight was as familiar and as soothing to Timothy as his own boredom. He and Laurence were in the habit of spending hours on end in the Arizona Cafe, after school hours; sometimes during them, too.

This afternoon – it was to be the last of its kind for Timothy; its indolence and vague expectancy were overnight to become more distant from him than all the tremors and revelations of his childhood – passed like the rest. They played cards with a couple of other boys from school who came in. They talked. They smoked. Laurence cleaned his fingernails with a broken match. He was an inveterate cleaner of his nails, which remained inveterately dirty. The lights inside the cafe were switched on; then those in the road outside it. Dusk brought more traffic into the street. It was time to be going home. Timothy walked first to Laurence's house: in the hope, which he did not divulge to Laurence, of seeing his sister Susie. Like some darkly living substance, the twilight enfolded every noise and every moving or stationary light that pierced it, and yet managed to remain whole.

Susie was not to be seen. Laurence did not invite him into the house. Timothy walked on.

Now he stands at the gate to the little front garden of his house. A light burns in the hall. There will be a smell of cooking, he knows, when he opens the front door. His mother will call out from the kitchen, 'Is that you, Timmee?' and he will answer, 'No, it's Santa Claus.'

For the moment, however, he lingers at the gate. The coming of evening has filled his breast with familiar yearnings and elations, a desire to take into his hands some soft, vulnerable creature and crush it out of sheer tenderness. Waiting outside the house he gives the world its last chance to justify the emotions it has roused in him.

Nothing happens. He can express both his hope and its disappointment only by bursting with an especially noisy cheerfulness through the front door.

No smell of cooking greets him. No call from his mother. In spite of the light burning in the hall, the house is empty.

There is a note on the single drawer of the hallstand. It reads, in Maureen's hopelessly unskilled hand: *Have gone to Keep appointment at Hospital, help yourself to Cold meat and Tomatoe in Lardar.*

Maureen had made only the most modest demands of life. The demands life made of her, before it finally let her go, were extravagant. Her body bowed under their pressure. Her face buckled. Even her nose was twisted to one side. Her shoulders were pulled in towards one another. A hump grew between her shoulder blades. Her chin was drawn to her chest. Her body shrank.

Yet when she lay on her side, curled into herself, it was strange how much bulkier than before she appeared to be, like an animal crouched to sleep.

Presently she would be seen to be awake, blinking, lying always with her face turned to the window.

From outside Timothy and Gerhard could never tell which was her window, among all those punched out of the template of the hospital wall. Above it was the sky, in which meaningless clouds assembled and dispersed, lights shone and went out, sounds gathered and were lost.

They brought her home. She had lived between peace and panic, moving easily from the one to the other, remembering little of what she left behind each time the passage was made. Now she was imprisoned in fear. She knew what was happening to her. She knew it was happening to her alone. From the beginning she never doubted what the end would be. She swallowed the drugs she was given, and submitted to the needles that were put into her. She went away in an ambulance and was placed under machines which hurled great bolts of radio-activity through her. The treatments made her nauseous, but she was too weak to bring up anything. Her bodily processes went on, though each seemed to take more from her than it gave in support or relief. Gerhard was a stunned, devoted nurse. Mrs Davis from The Sewing Basket came to visit her, puffed and panted up the stairs, gazed at the patient, and went away saying vaguely that you never could tell how things would work out. Mrs Robinson came, held Maureen's hand in her own, and asked Gerhard, in a loud whisper on her way out, if he didn't want her to call a priest. Gerhard said sharply, almost waspishly, that he did not. Even Mr Truter came, towards the end.

Timothy saw the visitors out at the front door. He

looked at them with a stare wider and emptier than his mother's had ever been. He spoke little. He did whatever Gerhard asked him to. At first he had childishly expected some ill-defined authority – medical most likely, but perhaps even political or charitable – to step in and bring the crisis to an end by restoring his mother to him, just as she used to be. None appeared. Instead it slowly became clear to him that death's authority over his mother was absolute. It had been so over every mother who had lived before her. The passage of the centuries made no difference to it. It would not resign from its position. It was not to be diverted. It never looked up from its work. It was utterly incorruptible. Only flesh was corruptible, in every sense of the word. That was why death took up its domicile within it.

Maureen's mind began to wander. She spoke to her dead mother and to friends from her childhood. She became more confused than before when she found that these phantoms seemed to have forgotten so much of what she wanted to find out from them. She continually demanded to know what day of the week it was, imagining that everything would become quite clear to her once she was told; then she repeated the answers she was given like the names of foreign cities, to which she had been transported without her knowledge. She called Gerhard to ask him who Timothy was, and asked Timothy who Gerhard was. She got up several times with a sudden access of energy and purpose that left her stranded on the edge of her bed, examining her hands as if she might find, among their protruding bones and loose skin, what she had set out to look for. Her voice became more and more faint;

towards the end she moved her lips in the belief that she was speaking, while her eyes anxiously scanned the faces of the people around her for an answer to the words she was incapable of uttering.

One night, when Timothy sat next to her bed, and Gerhard was asleep in the next room, she beckoned him to come closer to her. She took his head in her hands and brought it down to her breast, which smelled overpoweringly of drugs and dissolution. She put the point of her chin on the top of his head, and pressed down hard on it.

Gerhard found them in one another's arms the next morning. Maureen's body was cold. So was Timothy's. For a moment Gerhard thought that Timothy had killed his mother with an overdose, and then taken his own life. But he opened his eyes at Gerhard's shout. Gerhard collapsed into the chair next to the bed, and put his head in his hands. Timothy got up from where he had been lying, half on the bed and half on the floor. He crossed the room to look through the window on to Omdurman Terrace. The yellow sodium streetlamps were still burning, though there was no longer any need for them. The first sunbeam of the morning already quivered against the chimney stack of the house opposite, as if trying to finger the brickwork loose. It succeeded: the edges of the chimney suddenly became molten and streamed away, leaving a black mark standing like a half-submerged rock in the middle of the cascade. All along the road much the same thing was happening to other edges and ledges. But the sun rose in one place only, quite quickly.

Later, at Gerhard's request, Timothy walked

over to the doctor's surgery, to tell him of Maureen's death. It was going to be a windless spring morning of dark sunlight and pallid shadows: a world inverted, or turned peacefully inside out. Timothy walked through the streets in which he had passed his blank, squirming infancy, his childhood, his degraded boyhood. Here a terrace of pebble-dash houses turned away from him and fled downhill; there, between low shop fronts, a double-decker bus moved cautiously, as if the driver was afraid of knocking over the child-size constructions around him. Here was the doctor's surgery; and here, his once overpowering face now subverted by many wrinkles, was the doctor who had been attending to the family for so many years. He expressed his regret at Timothy's news, and said he would be over at the house soon; he looked sharply at Timothy and asked if *he* was all right. Timothy said he was. And his father? He was all right too. They were both all right. Only his mother was dead.

Another sharp look from the doctor was lost on Timothy, who was already opening the door to the street. Once he was out on the pavement he did not know which way to go. Eventually he turned in the direction of the house. No school for him today.

No school for him tomorrow, either. He was never to go to school again.

When Gerhard and Timothy arrived at the crematorium, smoke was already emerging from a corner of the great square chimney of the building. Not Maureen's, they were assured: they hadn't come too late. The smoke wavered, bent, bowed over, hung motionless, seemed to squat down grossly upon itself, then suddenly rose, stretching out long fingers that quivered helplessly before their disappearance into the space that always remained just above their reach. Vanishing, they did not perceptibly thicken the haze over the entire suburb; they did nothing to darken the faint, silvery rays which the sun, hidden behind cloud, sent out across the sky.

A few minutes later that was the way Maureen had gone. She too had ridden those rays. Goodbye, Maureen! Dispersed forever over the London she belonged to, she was free to sift down on to the leaves of suburban trees; to speck the windows of cars queuing up at traffic lights; to be dusted off bookcases by houseproud women; to be washed off the hands and knees of children in sportive, lukewarm baths; to fall into crevices between tile and beam, or cracks in Portland stone, and remain there.

Her son and widower made their way out of the building. Its courtyards and ivy-hung walls gave it a deceptively collegiate appearance. It even had wooden doors studded with large, quasi-medieval bolts. Cars kept pulling into and departing from a gravelled car park. Above, a cloud moved, the sun flashed momentarily, and its rays shifted with a boom-like sweep of light across the sky. But not in Maureen's honour.

For several years before Maureen's death Gerhard had been making his living less by painting pictures of his own than by dealing in the pictures and furniture of others. The development had seemed natural enough. At first he had conducted his business from the house; later he had rented a small shop off a main street in Wood Green. From the outside of his shop one might have supposed that he specialised in dust, coal scuttles, coronation mugs, and battered sets of the Children's Encyclopaedia.

The Sewing Basket, where Maureen had worked, was a more genteel affair. In its window a female mannequin swathed in lengths of curtaining stared out at the street, to which she also extended one chipped hand. Behind her there radiated a sunburst of rods with innumerable balls of wool skewered upon them, like multi-coloured, six-foot kebabs. Inside the shop, on a wooden chair, her immense, brown-stockinged legs crossed beneath her with the effect of an arrested flow or ooze, sat Mrs Davis, ready at all times to issue advice and instructions to customers and assistants alike.

After his mother's death Timothy took her place in The Sewing Basket. He had had a Saturday morning job there for some years. Now he came several times a week. He cleaned, he shifted boxes about, he climbed up a little ladder to bring down bolts of cloth from the higher shelves, he carried the mannequin out of the window and put new funerary wrappings on her hairless pink body. It wasn't really a young man's work, Mrs Davis said, particularly when she saw him at that last task, but she was nevertheless glad to have him. He learned much about wool, cottons, knitting needles, buttons, trimmings, bias bindings; he was able to snap out a yard of cloth with the greatest despatch, measure it against a metal rule sunk into the counter, fold it over and snap out another, while his attention was apparently elsewhere.

The rest of the time he was on his own. Literally so. The house had been given up. The furniture had been sold (some of it from Gerhard's shop). Timothy and his father had gone into separate digs. Gerhard spent all day in his shop, staying there long after he had closed the doors in the evenings, browsing aimlessly among the bric-à-brac he had collected. He had also started painting again, in the back room behind the shop; he filled canvas after canvas with mourning female figures of a gauzy allegorical type, storm-clouds well in evidence above their veiled heads. He sometimes even slept in that room, on a brokendown chaise longue he had bought as part of a job lot.

Timothy had accepted all these arrangements without demur. He had other preoccupations. The books he was reading. The yoga positions he tried to adopt after studying illustrations of them. The food and sleep he deliberately went without, in order to see what would be revealed to him as a result. The meanings he tried to cull from flights of birds, patterns of cars parked in the street outside his room, snatches of words overheard in buses, clues to crosswords in the morning's paper. He was ready at all times to receive important messages that were being transmitted to him alone.

Why not? Who else was there to receive them? Who would believe what he had remembered to be the truth about himself? He was eighteen years old. In a few weeks' time the boys he had been at school with would be writing their A-level examinations. He had intended writing those exams too. Now he had more pressing problems to solve. It seemed to him that he didn't have all that much time in which to solve them. Time itself had become a most important problem to him. He spent much of it lying on his bed, thinking about it. He tried especially to get time past to call him back to itself. (This was quite a different process from him or anyone else trying to recall it.) Why should it be supposed that time was necessarily abolished, annihilated, once it was left behind? Perhaps Maureen was still there, he was still there, where they had been together. But if time past had an existence somehow independent of his recall of it, then presumably the same was true of time future. How could he get a ticket to it? By living? Was that the only way?

It became a habit with him to gaze at one or another part of his body for so long that whatever he was looking at ceased to have function or meaning, like a word repeated too many times. He saw instead stones shaped by secret currents, fields of hair bowed over in one direction like grass in a wind, lines that curved and ran into one another after the fashion of Arabic writing. Then he lost his way among these phenomena and found his body again. It was still lying in bed. Or it was walking about in the streets. It was working in The Sewing Basket. It was talking to Laurence Sendin or some of the other boys from school. It belonged to him. Timothy. Fearer of God. Son of Maureen and Gerhard Fogel. Living in the Borough of Hornsey. That didn't mean he wasn't entitled to ask hard questions. Or that he wasn't marked out for a hard fate . Everyone had to be just someone, and to be somewhere, anywhere, at one time or another. Again and again, in his mind's eye he slid open the bronze doors behind which a furnace raged, howled, drew in breath, drew in Maureen. He should have gone too! Then he would have achieved the immortality which was now hers. No, not hers: its. Always its. It that had been her. It that was still him.

As the molecules in a cooling liquid are 'fixed' into the solid, the tendency of the remainder to join them becomes greater and greater, until it finally becomes irresistible, leading to a sharp, cooperative phase transition. That's the analogy I must hang on to. If you want a large perfect crystal to occur in such conditions, it's obvious that the atoms or molecules should find very few centres to cohere around. No agitation, in other words. No irregularities in the containing vessel. Then only do they fall into ordered array.

So – patience. Whether you have it or not. Also confidence: on the same terms. To he who pretends shall be given.

Over her son's protests, Mrs Sendin brought out the big scrapbook of cuttings. In the Sendins' house for the very first time, seated at the living room table, Timothy turned over the glue-stiffened pages with great care, lest one stick to another and some of the precious yellowing clippings on the pages be defaced. On the far side of the table was a glass-fronted cabinet with silver cups and shields on display inside it. The doors of the cabinet were composed of small oblong panes held together by strips of lead, as in a church window or some other holy place.

SENDIN SENDS 'EM DOWN (*Evening Star.*) SENDIN SKITTLES NORTHANTS

(*Daily Telegraph*.) SENDIN TRIUMPH (*News Chronicle*.) 'Sendin's mastery was demonstrated once again at Taunton, where his inswingers pinned down Somerset on a wicket that should have given them many easy runs . . .' (*The Manchester Guardian*.)

There it was. In this room, which he had never before been invited to enter, but which he had pictured for himself so many times, Timothy found a life that had been transformed into objects: papers, silverware, nickelplate. He shivered inwardly at the thought which came to him from time to time with the insidiousness of a temptation: that there were no accidents in the world.

Laurence ostentatiously read the newspaper to show how indifferent he was to the display being put before the guest. He continued to read the paper when his father appeared. A car smash, time, and too much beer had transformed the former bowler of inswingers into a thick, limping man with a dent across his forehead and the back of his grey head, where an official, stiff-peaked, red-badged cap rested all day. When he opened his mouth to smile shamefacedly at the sight of the scrapbooks, Timothy saw most of Susie's crooked teeth, miraculously enlarged and tobacco-stained. Mr Sendin took his tea and retired conversationless into a corner. Mrs Sendin made no attempt to follow him into it. She sat at the table with Timothy, who gazed as long as he could at each page before him, hoping Susie would come in before he had to leave.

At last! In her school outfit she was dimmed, almost annulled, between the glow of childhood and the fierce flame of the adult. It's a trick that some girls have: so that your sight will be all the more darkened and dazzled when the breath of time suddenly makes them blaze up again.

But Timothy wasn't fooled. Her wan skin, the schoolgirl spots on her forehead, the awkwardness of her gesture when she saw him sitting there, the unflattering buckle which held her hair together behind her neck – he saw through them all. She was still his Susie. The possessor of his possessions.

A suffocating smell of hot wool came from the tea-cosy which sheathed the teapot. Mr Sendin had opened the jacket of his blue, curator's uniform; its buttons lowered their heads, hanging down from little brass loops. Susie said, 'No thanks mum, I don't want any tea.' She went out of the room, but returned almost immediately, wearing a pair of horn-rimmed glasses which were too large and heavy for the size of her face. Now that she could see him more clearly, she was friendlier to Timothy than she had been before, and called him Tommy. Nobody corrected her. Laurence merely smiled. He had put the paper aside and sat leaning forward, his knees apart, his hands hanging between them.

They were a cold lot, the Sendins. There were sly resemblances among them which became visible when they spoke to one another, and uncannily disappeared in repose. Mrs Sendin, the former neighbourhood expert in pooffy-poofs, asked Timothy, 'Does your father deal in old clothes too?'

Laurence answered her, before Timothy could speak. 'No, he doesn't.' Then, before she could speak: 'If you've got some stuff to sell you'll just have to wait until Charlie Barley comes around, like you always do.'

'I wasn't asking about – I wasn't asking for myself,' Mrs Sendin said, flustered at having to make the denial.

'Oh, I thought you were,' Laurence answered laconically.

Timothy sat among them like a specimen. The room was neat and shining. After the orphaned solitude, the empty disorder and confinement of the room he was living in, he felt himself to be under the scrutiny of many eyes. On one arm of every armchair was a small, highly polished brass ashtray, like a wrist watch, clipped on to a leather strap that hung down on each side to a weighted, fringed end. Under the chairs castor marks were indented forever on carpets and floorboards.

So many families! So many ways of growing older! Everyone has to have a place of shelter somewhere. Hence the incurable sadness of domesticity.

Only Laurence's room was untidy. It smelled of oil like a garage. Open wooden boxes, full of tools, machine parts, bits of meccano, and nuts and screws of all sizes, stood on shelves he had put up around the walls. His dirty fingers had a way with them. He tried to repair old radios. He pottered about with generators and motors. His chief love, however, was for locks. Other people's locks as well as his own. He listened to them, he responded to the lift and subsidence of their inner weights, he coaxed them towards the decisions he knew they were capable of coming to. He was like a confessor or counsellor to them; sometimes like a lover, when he stroked and penetrated them with his wires and stiff strips of plastic. Even while he was saying despairingly to Timothy, 'You see why I don't like bringing people here! You see what a crappy family I've got! Christ, I've just got to get out!' – even then his fingers were wandering among possessions, moving them about, making them clink gently together.

'I don't know,' Timothy said. 'They don't seem so bad to me.'

The file Laurence had been holding dropped into its box with a sharp, conclusive ring. The room was silent. 'Well –' he admitted grudgingly, 'my old man would be all right, except that he's half dead.'

When they went downstairs once again, the living room was empty. The tea things were gone. Looking anxiously around as he followed Laurence out of the house, knowing that time was fast running out on him, Timothy saw Susie's empty spectacle case on the table in the hall.

His hand moved of its own accord. It slipped the case into his pocket.

Imagine the difficulty of being an ordinary young man, with an ordinary young man's ambitions and desires, and finding yourself saddled with supernatural gifts.

No, that's not right. Supernatural hankerings would come closer to the truth. Or supernatural recollections.

After years of amnesia, Timothy had remembered the miraculous transmutations of himself of which he had been capable during his childhood. The recollection had come when he had struggled to be admitted

101

into his dying mother's body. To share in her death. To take her death into himself and to be taken into it, and so to release them both from its finality.

Nothing had happened. She had died. She had been burned. Dispersed. He had been orphaned. Twice orphaned, indeed. He had lost her, and he had been cast out into a world whose multifarious surfaces and depths were all equally alien to him. Everywhere he turned they excluded him. Unless . . .

All right, the rest of us have been there too. Still are there. With no conditional exits or alternatives.

But he couldn't forget for a second time that his relationship to the physical world (and hence to the world of spirit) had once been quite different from what it now appeared to be. The memory was as insubstantial as a cloud trailing between sea and sky, a fringe of rain which could be a mere illusion of glare and distance, gone when you look for it again. It was also as intimate and ever-present as his hand. It could not be severed from him. He did not know which aspect of it frightened him more. Often he told himself that what he remembered had never been anything more than a childish dream, to which there could be no return. As often, the vision of a life stripped of the kind of possibility that had once been proffered to him, the desolation of having no alternative selves or modes of existence to look forward to, was more than he could bear. To be what he was for all time (or no time), to waive forever the prospects of transfiguration – no, it might be possible for others to live like that. He couldn't. He wouldn't. He wasn't meant to.

One speculation always led to another. The noise of

traffic and passing trains contributed to the endless debate. Children shouted out what sounded like their contribution to it while they kicked balls about in open spaces. Dogs turned their heads interrogatively towards him. Any window frame or door handle or discarded tyre or piece of brickwork which he allowed his eye to rest on presented itself to him as a challenge, a plea, and a lure.

First things first. Timothy came to a decision. Having finished work early one afternoon, he did not turn home as he usually did, but walked straight downhill to his father's shop.

Gerhard made him welcome by retiring into the scullery just off the back room, where he washed out a couple of cups and saucers and put a kettle on to boil. Then he seated himself directly in front of Timothy, on a slippery wooden chair with a straight back and swollen ankles. To make himself more secure, he twisted his own ankles behind those of the chair, and clutched its seat in the V between his open legs.

These arrangements concluded, he smiled and asked what he could do for Timothy today.

Upright on the chaise longue, holding Susie's spectacle case in his jacket pocket, Timothy was tempted to answer, 'Nothing. Obviously. How can you do anything for me? I hardly know you. You're sitting in such an uncomfortable position. You have such a funny, brown, tilted face. I'm surprised your glasses don't fall off. I don't even know if you're my father.'

But he kept all these remarks to himself. He had

103

come to make a confession. To carry out an experiment. Shiftily, in a low voice, with many pauses, slowly turning over and over the object hidden in his hand, looking from Gerhard to the gilt-framed mirror that hung at an angle from the wall and that held to its flat, glassy bosom an inverted view of the shop through the doorway, he told Gerhard what he wanted.

Gerhard listened attentively. Occasionally he changed the angle at which he kept his head. Occasionally he sniffed. His expression was grave. He asked few questions.

When Timothy had finished, Gerhard left him in the disorder of the back room and went into the shop. With a trembling hand he dusted a set of Doulton china that might have been valuable if the set had been complete, and if each of the surviving members of it had been so too. Leaning against a sideboard he paused to scrutinise, without taking in anything of what he was reading, an article about corals from an illustrated, leather-bound Victorian volume on natural history. Finally he stood in the door of his shop and looked up and down the street. The brightest objects in sight were the trays of fruit, raked back like seats in a theatre, that had been put out on the pavement by the greengrocer opposite. He too was standing idly in his doorway, and waved to Gerhard, who responded with a more dignified gesture. A milk float passed down the road, a clanking lorry, several cars. The noise they made was suddenly overwhelmed by that of a jet plane overhead: magnified by the clouds, its roar was an arch or dome of sound that swelled enormously to fill all the available space, before instantly transforming itself into a silken cloth being drawn through an ever-diminishing ring. An old lady, pushing a wheeled shopping basket and holding two puppies on a leash, stopped to look at Gerhard's window. Gerhard folded his arms and raised his chin to show that he was not looking for her custom. The entanglement of wheels, legs, paws, and connections between them moved on, leaving behind mysterious, retaliatory emanations of displeasure. Gerhard consulted his watch. Surely he had given the boy long enough. On the other hand it wouldn't do to rush matters. Not with something as important as this.

Still debating with himself, he crept as quietly as he could into the room. He approached Timothy who was lying on his side on the chaise longue, his forehead against one of the balustrade-like supports to the back-rest of the piece. Gerhard stood over him for a moment, before he lowered his hand.

Timothy sat up. Vaguely he pushed his father from him. He shook his head, as if waking from sleep, and stared blankly forward. His eyes met Gerhard's.

'Well?' he asked.

Gerhard was silent. Apologetically, he said, 'I don't know. You were too quick for me. I couldn't be sure.'

'Didn't you feel – anything?'

'Yes, I think I did. Perhaps I did.'

'What?'

'Well, I don't know. I think I did feel that you were . . . harder. Perhaps . . . cooler, also. I'm sure, cooler. I noticed that. It was remarkable. For a moment.'

'Did you really?'

'I think so, yes.'

'You're just saying it because you think that's what

I want to hear.'

'No, no, no. How could I? Your own father! About such an important matter! I'm telling you, Timothy, that you did feel – somehow – I'm not sure . . . different.'

'You don't believe me.'

Timothy said no more for several minutes. Gerhard watched him closely, then crossed the room and sat down in front of a writing bureau which served as his desk, his filing cabinet, his overnight safe, and his luncheon table. It was also for sale.

'You think nothing happened. That I stayed just the same as before,' Timothy said to his back.

'What do *you* think?' Gerhard asked, as if trying to find a confederate in guilt.

'I don't know,' Timothy confessed. 'If you don't know, then I don't know either.'

Gerhard turned to him, dropping the paper clip he had been playing with. 'So? That's good. Excellent! What do you want of yourself? You should be pleased. Now you needn't let this business worry you any more. You can forget about it! You forgot about it last time, when you were a little boy – isn't that right? So now it should be easier for you to do it again.'

'You just want me to be ordinary!' Timothy cried.

'Ach,' Gerhard answered, trying to set aside with a single, penitential sweep of his arm all the dreams he had nourished on Timothy's behalf, 'who can be so lucky nowadays?'

I had an unexpected guest for dinner tonight. My dear papa, come all the way from London on a flying visit. Not to see me. Oh no, of course not. He'd come on business. He'd come because he wanted to consult Dr Wuchs about his health. And then, only then, while he was about it, to see me.

We met in the foyer. He held out both hands to me and we embraced. Then we stood at arms' length and looked at one another. We were both much moved. He smiled – I knew so well the movement of the skin around his eyes! – and he said, 'My dear boy, how are you? Feeling better, I hope?'

'Definitely.'

Every gesture he made, every wrinkle on his skin, could surprise me only by the intimacy with which I knew it. Yet, for a few minutes, I was also able to see him with the eyes of a relative stranger. Trapped within the shaven, scented expanses of his face, I could see the baby he must once have been. It was a baby who looked out through his big, shiny brown eyes; who lifted the curve of his little nose, at once delicate and coarse, and sniffed the air for any hint of danger or disapproval; who turned down the corners of his mouth in the traditional pout of the spoiled child.

And I heard him with a stranger's ears. In his speech Leipzig lingers. With an overlay of his Leipzig notions of an English gentleman's turn of phrase. My dear fellow . . . nothing would please me more . . . I wouldn't dream of it . . . how absurd . . . you are too kind . . .

Going out to dinner we ran into Marnie. I introduced them to each other. He put himself out to be pleasant. He always does with strangers. When we left her to go to my table: 'So you are finding some amusement here? As well as . . . rest . . . therapy?'

I smiled mysteriously. Actually, poor Marnie and I have done nothing more than have the occasional cup of coffee together.

We ate outside on the terrace. He began immediately to sing the praises of Dr Wuchs. How glad he was that I'd agreed to put myself in his hands. How sure he was that I'd benefit from his treatments. What a wonderful man he was in every respect.

'Unorthodox, of course. But truly original. Full of insight. He did a lot for me at a time when things were very difficult indeed, when I didn't know where to turn.'

His plump, black-haired hands fluttered; drooping eyelids hooded his gaze momentarily. 'I mean, of course, when your mother . . .'

'I know.'

'And discreet! Utterly, utterly . . . You mustn't be inhibited in any way by the thought that he and I . . . that anything you would want to keep private would ever . . .'

'In other words, the two of you have already been talking about me.'

His injured, baby eyes widened. 'Should I deny it? I asked him how you were getting on. He told me you were making progress. We agreed that you are a most interesting but also' – he touched my arm protectively – 'a rather difficult young man. He said that it had been a privilege for him to get to know you. And then, if you'll forgive me, we talked of my concerns, not yours. He examined me. I've had one or two symptoms I wanted to mention to him while I was here. Feelings of pressure, nothing more. A certain lassitude. He was most reassuring.'

He tackled his grape-fruit. It was evening: the warmest, I think, since I've been here. The little cypress trees in tubs around the edge of the terrace had already lost their daytime shades of green and were wholly black, as flat as silhouettes. But some light still hung on in the sky. A passing plane, high overhead, trailed silver plumes brighter than its mote-like self.

I asked after my stepmother. Papa assured me, with another inexplicably reproachful movement of the eyes, that she was fine, fine. Having despatched his grape-fruit, he turned to the *truite au four*. It didn't take him long. His knife and fork moved nimbly about the plate, sorting and separating, pausing for brief, nose-down inspections of what they turned up. Then squash-and-carry. When there was nothing edible left on the plate, he wiped the corners of his mouth with his napkin.

'Very good. I was hungry. They gave me nothing to eat on the way here.'

It grew darker. Though the plane was long gone, its vapour trails were still visible overhead: they had broadened and were mingling together; their colour had changed from silver to bronze. While we waited for the fillet, he told me about the piece of business which had brought him from London. It was a nice little picture, a sketch by a pupil of Claude's, well-authenticated and characteristic in style, almost a *trompe l'oeil,* with the lines of a tree like a vague cloud in the foreground and a cloud as precise as a tree in the sky behind it. The owner, an old acquaintance, had to get rid of it quietly and rapidly, for reasons which he had gone into at length, and which might possibly have been his real reasons. So papa had made him an offer; he was waiting for a phone call to hear whether or not it had been accepted. Then he'd be leaving for London immediately. There was a plane at ten fifteen. He had to be back tonight.

He took the fillet of beef more slowly. We didn't have anything to drink on the table, apart from a bottle of Perrier water. Neither of us is a drinking man. That's one of the characteristics we have in common. A waiter tossed a salad for us. Lights had been burning inside the dining room for some time; now those out here on the terrace were also turned on. At once shadows appeared at sly angles to every object in sight, including the heap of sauté potatoes on my plate; the voices of the diners around us rose in volume; a degree of theatricality affected even the cypresses in their tubs, which promptly began to gleam and bristle as if on parade.

Papa responded in his own way, too. He lowered his head, he looked sideways at me, he brought the back of his little finger to his mouth, and asked me from behind it, in a voice that was tenderly pitched just above a whisper, 'Tell me the truth, are you really feeling better? Have you thrown off those . . . those . . .'

'Attacks?' I helped him out with the word. And with another: 'Delusions?'

He nodded.

So did I. Then, before he had time to take pleasure in my nod, I said, 'They've been replaced by something worse, in a way.'

His eyes jumped. 'What? What do you mean?'

'I'll show you. After dinner.'

There followed a depressed silence for the assimilation of what I'd said. For the arrival of coffee. The deepening of shadows around us. The removal with a toothpick of the last shreds of filet mignon between papa's teeth.

'Have you spoken to Dr Wuchs about this? Whatever it is – that you've just mentioned.'

'No.'

'Why not, for heaven's sake?' He seized on this as a legitimate excuse for the vexation he felt. 'You must take him into your confidence absolutely. Otherwise you're just wasting your time here. And you're wasting money too. No-one begrudges the money – that goes without saying – but I'm entitled to know that you're taking full advantage of what it brings you.' His broad shoulders, white collar, and darkened jowls had come right over the table towards me; now they retreated. He looked all about the terrace in an aggrieved manner, apparently expecting the others on it to come to his support. They went on eating and drinking. He said despondently. 'If you don't like it here, if you don't think there's any point in staying on, then perhaps you should simply come back home with me. Tonight. We – you – can try something else.'

'No, I don't want to go. I want to finish the work I'm doing.'

'What work?'

'You'll see.'

'When?'

'After dinner.'

'This work – it's the same thing that you were talking about a moment ago?'

'You'll see.'

I was enjoying myself: I must admit it. Poor papa! He was already distressed, I knew, at what I'd said; he would be even more distressed, I was sure, when he read the pile of obsessed scribblings I had to show him upstairs. That he should be transformed into poor, meek, daubing Gerhard in Hornsey; that the dim, water-green depths of Joachim's, where mirrors in acanthus-leaf frames reflect indiscriminately the gloom and glitter of lacquered chests and screens, jewels, enamels, ivory and glass, as if in some Victorian genre painting ('The Sunken Indiaman') – that his beloved gallery should be transformed into Gerhard's squalid second-hand shop; that my spirited

112

Anglo-Irish mother should be degraded into proletarian Maureen; that the property king and patron of the arts with whom she had bolted shortly before her death should figure in my 'memoirs' as rent-collecting, handy Mr Truter . . . I could imagine how deeply distasteful papa would find it all. Was *that* how I chose to see him? Was that how I rewarded him for so many years of paternal indulgence and affection? Did I have no respect for his achievement in creating his life and career anew after the flight from Germany; no appreciation of the elegant and interesting social circle in which he moved, and into which he had been proud to introduce his only son? And what about my own view of myself, as revealed in my writings? How little self-respect was it possible for a man to have!

I felt he had waited long enough. We got up to go, leaving our napkins in white heaps next to the empty cups and saucers. Now: the truth. What did I feel as I walked through the lounge, along the corridor towards the stairs? Nothing much. In the corridor we passed illuminated glass cases containing bottles of perfume, watches, and silk scarves, with the names of shops above them. We went up in a lift that sighed and wheezed like an old chain-smoker, and smelled like the inside of his mouth. We marched along another broad, deserted corridor, much less well lit than those below. The sadness of hotel corridors! The shabby mystery of all their closed doors! I needn't enlarge on such obvious themes. I wouldn't even mention them, were it not that they were clearly weighing on papa's mind as he walked along by my side. He was plainly nervous of what might be waiting for him at the end of our promenade. Who could blame him? At last we reached my door. I opened it. The light had been left burning inside. 'Do go through,' I said, inviting him to precede me. He did so, a little gingerly. From the back there was nothing babyish about his appearance: it was that of a bent, ageing, tonsured man, with a fringe of grey hair that reached down to his jacket collar.

'Well?'

It was the first word he had said since we had left the table.

I opened the drawer in which I keep my papers when I'm not working on them. I brought out the whole pile and put it in his hands.

'You can sit on the couch,' I said. 'Here, I'll switch on the reading lamp for you.'

He didn't follow my suggestion, perhaps because something about the room had made him uneasy, perhaps because he was so eager to solve the riddle I'd been teasing him with. Standing in the middle of the room, he took his rimless glasses out of his pocket, and shook the shafts open with a gesture rather like that of a doctor with a thermometer. Wearing glasses made him look weaker and older. Even poorer, somehow. He started to examine the page on top of the pile, but broke off at once to bring it closer to his face. He frowned, glanced in my direction, then stood quite still, his gaze resting neither on me nor on the page before him. There was an expression of bafflement, even of despair, on his face. From the effort he had to make when he lifted the papers to look at them again, one might have thought they had suddenly become much heavier than before. (Yet how gently the whole sheaf breathed in and exhaled as he did it!) He turned over the next three or four pages with no more than the briefest glance at each. Finally he chose one at random from the middle of the pile and studied it for a little longer than he had the others. The bewilderment on his face had given way to apprehension; then I saw nothing but pain or pity there. Even his colour had changed. It was less swarthy-pink now; more browny-grey.

'Very amusing,' he said unexpectedly.

His voice was hoarse. He handed the papers back to me.

'Aren't you going to read them?'

Clearing his throat before he was able to bring the words out, he repeated, 'Very amusing.'

He left immediately. I saw him down the stairs and into the foyer. At the desk he enquired whether there had been a call for him. The youth behind it deigned to tell him that there hadn't been. He gave instructions for any caller to be told that he had already left for London. A taxi was summoned; it came almost immediately. We did not embrace on parting. His last words, when he was already sitting in the car, were, 'You must trust Dr Wuchs. If he can't help you I just don't know –!' His hands opened and fell into his lap. He was still wearing his glasses. I stood on the steps of the hotel and watched the taxi go. I waited there until I could no longer hear the sound of its engine.

The little lights to the side of the tarmac flick by, alternately orange and green: each in its housing strangely peaceful in appearance, almost pastoral, at a distance from the next. Beyond, in and around the terminal buildings, other lights swarm together in fiercely incandescent clusters and layers that give to the darkness the one slowly moving horizon it has.

A pause. A vibration. A discreet but ever more insistent howl. The plane gathers speed, the lights flash past more and more rapidly, until at last they blur, they stream into lines, into narrow, multi-coloured torrents. At any moment now they will be gone, fallen into black gulfs of air, left far behind.

That's how it must be for papa, going home. That's how I feel it to be with me, too. Everything has become a flowing, a rushing, a silent roaring. These lines speed by. No braking now. No sorting one from another. It's too late. They'd scream if I tried to bring them to a halt.

Timothy prayed. Not in words. The god he wanted to reach wasn't interested in words. Only in achieved states. Palpable transformations. Proven exceptions. The certain resolution of contradictions. He came into being with them. He would be known only by those who had gone through them. He was not to be confused with subjective sensations. His was the spirit redeemed by its own efforts from its entanglement with matter. His were the virtues of matter – gravity, conductivity, predictability – bestowed upon spirit. He was eternity humanised. The individual consciousness eternised. Flesh and blood held secure from decay. Memory made tangible. Thoughts occupying space.

119

Inevitably, Timothy's prayers sometimes degenerated into random fantasies of which he felt ashamed because he was apparently so little capable of realising even the simplest among them. To become rich, of course. But far more than that. To make stone talk, wood walk, steel weep. Transform gestures into music. Brass into gold. Command a tea-spoon to leap into life and begin stirring his tea simply by pointing a finger at it. Kill through thought. Revive the dead. Abolish space for oneself but not for others. Hold up the future indefinitely, or make it come long before anyone expected it to. Play back the past like a spool of film or reel of tape. Read minds. Better still: read minds, and change their contents as one read, as if with an irritable authorial pen...

And so on and on, until words were once again left behind, and he wandered through wide inner areas of indistinction, groping with eyes that did not see, hands that did not feel, a mind that had abandoned thought, after a power that could be reached and seized in no other way.

For the failure of the experiment he had conducted in his father's shop (and it had been a failure; he couldn't pretend otherwise) Timothy blamed himself. He had erred in trying to go back instead of forward. He had attempted merely to duplicate the revelations of his childhood, instead of trying to establish what would be demanded of him and given back to him as an adult. He did not repeat that experiment, either on his own or in the company of others.

He took no-one into his confidence. Only god: the exacting and innovative god he was determined to bring into being.

But the real magician, it seemed was Laurence Sendin. He made diamond rings, silver bracelets, and gold brooches, out of nothing.

How?

Like this. Humming absently, his eyes for once less restive than his hands, he goes about his work. In a vacant house that smells of its own emptiness, that seems to listen intently to its own silence, in rooms that others have furnished for their eyes only, he is more alone than it is possible to be anywhere else in the world. There are letters lying in a heap inside the front door, where they have been shot through by the postman. The framed photographs of strangers stare at him from tables and walls with an imbecile helplessness. Nothing can compare with the strength and purposefulness his solitude gives him. He is surrounded by countless numbers of houses; they were built to keep him out; they will do it again tomorrow; an entire society has assembled itself around just that task. But his purpose is so much stronger than theirs that walls and locked doors now protect and conceal him, they set him free to do exactly what pleases him within them.

He moves quickly and deftly. Sometimes he pauses to listen to cars passing down the street, sometimes merely to let the silence of the house reassert itself. He opens drawers and searches through their contents, he forces open a writing bureau, he tips books from their shelves. Disorder accumulates behind him, household possessions are transformed instantly into litter, as he enters room after room. In a bleak spare bedroom, apparently the least used in the house, in the bottom drawer of a chest filled with linen, he finds what he is looking for. It is a small leather case, rather like a man's toilet bag. He zips it open. His face expressionless, he touches and turns over the bright, tinkling objects within it, then closes it again.

Cautiously, he stands to one side of the window and looks down at a back-garden vista of lawns, paling fences, trees about to lose their last leaves, tool sheds, wooden poles holding up washing lines adorned only by rows of roosting clothes-pegs. Television aeriels stick out like hearing aids from behind the chimneys of houses. A plastic ball rises into level rays of sunlight and falls out of them, to the cries of unseen children. The life of the people out there suddenly seems hateful to Laurence: it is so easy for them, yet it makes things so difficult for him. He goes to the front of the house to look down at the street, and decides it would be best for him to wait until dark before leaving. From information gathered beforehand he knows there is no chance of the owners of the house returning unexpectedly. There, on the big double bed, with its nylon counterpane and padded, buttoned headboard in yellow satin, he'll wait it out. On a table next to the bed is a photograph of a wedding party, in an ornate silver frame; the people in the picture are wearing clothes of a style fashionable before Laurence was born. Without getting up, without moving his feet from where they are propped up on the headboard, he rips the photograph out of the frame and throws it on the floor; the frame he keeps next to him on the bed, with the leather case. Time passes slowly. He watches the smoke of his cigarettes rise against the windows' illuminated oblongs. As it wanes, the glare of the sun through dusty glass becomes more and more bleared, and he becomes more melancholy and afraid. He wants to flee; also to burst into tears of self-pity. But he forces himself to remain where he is. It will soon be dark.

Before leaving, while the sun flares up for the last time among clouds as black as cinders, he conscientiously slits open with the blade of his clasp knife all the mattresses and cushions in the house. He isn't looking for anything that might be concealed in them. His own melancholy and bitterness seem sufficient justification for what he is doing. The fierce, solitary pride he had felt on coming into the house is gone; he doesn't believe it will ever return. The weight inside his jacket gives him no pleasure.

After a final scrutiny of the street, he steps firmly out of the front door, closes it behind him, and walks away. He does not look back. From streetlamp to streetlamp, faint shadows precede and follow him.

Timothy held on his lap the little leather bag Laurence had thrown at him. The smile with which he had done it was still on Laurence's lips. He watched Timothy closely.

'Can I look inside again?'

'Sure.'

Timothy unzipped the bag which he had closed hastily a few moments before, in the shock of seeing what it contained. Now he gazed at the treasures of metal and stone inside it, unable to take his eyes off

123

them. He had never held such things in his hands before. Anonymous and ownerless, they had been stripped of human irrelevancies by Laurence's agile fingers. They gleamed and rang tiny notes from each other every time they were moved. They were heavier than money.

He took out a ring, a gold ring, with a yellow, wine-coloured stone set in it. He didn't know the name of the stone. In shape it resembled a crown, bevelled and cut flat at the top, faceted at the sides. Its light was density; its density, light. Looking at the ring, Timothy felt a deep envy of Laurence, almost a hatred of him. He just did it! He acted. He changed his life. However laboriously, he got results.

'How long have you been doing this?'

'A few months. I've only done two jobs so far. The first one was a washout.'

'Aren't you scared?'

'Sometimes. But it's better than being so piss-scared you don't do anything at all. That's what most people are like.'

Laurence sounded very sure of himself. Over the last couple of years his face had acquired its grown-up shape: two sallow slabs of meat had been stuck on to his jowls. His dark hair was combed back. His shoulders had broadened.

He'd always been a thief. When he and Timothy had first become friends, he was already breaking into the cases and lockers of other boys at school. Later he had tried his hand at shoplifting. Now he had graduated. He was going to be cautious. He didn't intend to over-reach himself. He would carry on doing small jobs on his own, in the areas he knew well from his work as the driver of a laundry van, rather than go into partnership with others who might prove unreliable.

'Does Susie know?'

'Hell, no. Nobody knows. Except you.'

'Except me?' Timothy said, as if the distinction had been intended as an insult. 'What do you want – you want to cut me in?'

Laurence didn't take offence at his tone. 'No thanks, I don't fancy you on the job. You're much too dreamy.'

'Then why did you tell me about it?'

'You're my friend. So I told you.'

'Now I must think what a big shot you are?'

'If you like.'

They were both silent.

Timothy turned the ring in his hand, looking at the play of light inside it. Then he slipped it on to his little finger; it wouldn't go on any other. Again he turned it this way and that. The more light it gave off, the more it contained.

'It's probably just glass.'

'As long as the guy I sell it to doesn't know.'

A movement of the wrist and forearm, an ironic inflection of the voice: nothing more. Gone already. But the sudden resemblance between brother and absent sister affected Timothy painfully. He got up from the chair he had been sitting in, dropped the leather case on the bed, and walked to the window.

Window, chair, wardrobe, bed, table, walls, bookshelf: his room. His place of prayer. Where he schemed, night after night. His gaze went around the room once again. Laurence was sitting on the table. In one of the drawers beneath him was Susie's spectacle case. He was tempted to show it to Laurence; to show him that he wasn't the only one who could make something out of nothing. His one trophy! From constant handling the plastic skin of the case had begun to fray away at the edges and hinges, revealing the metal beneath. He could imagine Laurence's scorn and amusement if he did display it. And his disbelief: you mean, you and Susie –!

Wearily Timothy put his head against the glass. The curtains were drawn. It was a wet night. He looked into the winking darkness outside: beads of rain trying to get in through the glass; sodden leaves on paving stones below, and a puddle in the middle of the road wavering helplessly every time another drop fell into it.

'You know,' he said, still looking out, 'in India – in Tibet – places like that – there are holy men who can make that kind of stuff out of water. And sand, and manure. Just by praying and contemplating, they change it, they make jewels grow in the palms of their hands. Out of the little balls of mud they've rolled into shape. I've read about them in some of my books. There's even a special name for the things they produce. They're called *apports* . . .'

He turned to look at Laurence. 'Imagine doing that! What it must feel like. Just compare it with what you've done!'

'No,' Laurence said, quite respectfully. 'I leave that to you.'

Some minutes later he took the case from the bed, where Timothy had thrown it. He slipped it inside his windcheater. Then he remembered: 'My ring. Can I have that too?'

'Yours, is it?' Timothy said ironically. He was still at the window, half-sitting on the sill. He took the ring between thumb and forefinger, to ease it off.

It stuck fast. He couldn't get it over the first knuckle of his finger.

'Go on, get a move on,' Laurence urged him.

Timothy held out his hand. 'You get it off.'

Laurence tried. His dark head bent like a servant's over Timothy's hand. He tugged and turned and massaged both the ring and the finger. Timothy winced but made no protest. It was no good. The ring would not pass over the supple, obdurate swelling of bone, flesh, and wrinkled skin.

'You're bloody right,' Laurence said, between irritation and amusement. 'It's grown there.'

Timothy withdrew his hand and looked at the stone. It was as if he had donned a small, yellow, eternal flame, with a will of its own. The unexpectedness of the grip it had taken of him! The strength of it! Even while he was looking at it the stone changed colour, seeming to retreat into itself, growing darker and deeper. Then it came back towards him, all the brilliance of its gaze restored. Like his mother's. Had he not been so calm, he might have been greatly afraid and greatly excited. Instructions came in many forms. Possibilities were not to be anticipated. Eternities were everywhere, if only you had an eye for them.

Laurence was talking of getting the ring off with soap or grease. Timothy interrupted him.

'I think I should keep it.'

'Don't be daft! I can get it off – '

'I want to keep it.'

'Why, all of a sudden?'

'I don't know. I just do. I want to see what happens.' After a pause he said, 'I'll buy it from you.'

Laurence stared at him for a long time. Then he surrendered.

'If you really want it, you can have the damned thing. I'll give it to you.'

No more was said. Timothy did not even thank him. He saw Laurence down the stairs.

A few weeks later Timothy told Gerhard that he wanted to give up the job in The Sewing Basket and to come into his shop, instead.

I still haven't been able to work out why papa behaved so strangely the other evening. He knew absolutely nothing about the work I've been doing, except for what I'd said to him at dinner. When I gave him the chance to learn more, he couldn't wait to hand the papers back to me. Why? And why did he look at me in such a sickly fashion? How could he be so incurious and at the same time so disapproving? It makes no sense.

Part of my irritation with him, I know, springs from a disappointed hunger for praise. I was hoping he'd be impressed by my inventions, no matter how much he may have disliked them. I expected him to say, 'I didn't know you could write like this!' That would have been a fine sentence to hear from one's father! And: 'Have you ever thought of doing something in the literary line?' That would have been nice, too. Encouraging. I'm entitled to a little encouragement.

Especially when I think how badly everything else is going.

That new young doctor, for instance. It was all most peculiar. This morning while waiting for Dr Wuchs to arrive, I amused myself by rehearsing what would happen when I told him that I wanted to discontinue his treatments. I intended to let him know, straight out, that his injections made me dizzy, his diet disagreed with me, his company displeased me. Lying on my bed, I imagined just how red his face would go when he heard this; how the areas between its wrinkles would expand, while the wrinkles themselves became shallower. Wuchs tumescent! In a voice much smaller than usual he'd say that I must take care, he wasn't prepared to put up with insults, he'd insist on full payment for the entire course of treatment I had begun. Whereupon I would take out of my desk a single diamond, the best in my collection, and offer it to him on the palm of my hand. The sight of it would pacify him amazingly.

Then I had a better idea. As before, I imagined his face becoming more and more engorged, until his eyes look as if they are being squeezed out of it like pips from a fruit. I say, 'You're going to have a stroke.' He falls full length on the floor; I have to step smartly out of the way to make sure he doesn't fall on me. Blood comes out of his nose. I ring the bell. When the maid comes, I need do no more than point. Then I go downstairs and take a walk in the woods. The pine

130

needles whisper fragrant secrets to me. Here and there a sycamore grows among the pines, reminding me how broad and complicated in shape leaves can be: they don't all have to look like stiff hairs or lines, tied together in little switches. Because I don't want to go back until the mess in the room has been cleared up, I walk on further. What do these warning signs in German say? Who built this culvert under the path? Why this high brick wall – to keep me in or to keep out others?

I was just remarking (in my mind, of course) how the sunlight looked like true, burnished copper overhead, and green oxidised copper at the foot of the tree trunks, when there was a knock on my door. I called, 'Come in,' getting up from the bed and girding myself for the fatal confrontation with Dr Wuchs. But the doctor who came in was one I'd never seen before. He spoke English with a Scots accent; he introduced himself as Dr Buchan. I could see that he'd modelled himself on Dr Wuchs, whose pupil he must be: he had the same build as the older man, and some of his mannerisms and gestures. He gave me an injection, though I told him I definitely wished to bring the course of treatment to an end. 'We can't settle that now,' he said. It was all he would say. 'We'll have to discuss the matter further.'

It's all obvious enough. Wuchs has sensed what I feel about him. That's why he doesn't come to see me. He sends his underling instead, with whom I can't negotiate: a coward's way of dealing with a difficult situation.

Actually, I have certain suspicions about him which I might as well get off my chest right now.

131

The question is: What did he do with himself between 1939 and 1947?

I have tried to get an answer from him on that point several times; so far without success. Not that I've asked him about it directly. It would be hopeless to try. But I've managed to put together the chronology of his life pretty completely, one way and another. I know when he graduated, and when he did his postgraduate work at Johns Hopkins in the States, when he published his first paper . . . The years follow regularly upon each other until the outbreak of the Second World War. Then there's a sudden unexplained gap in the story. About everything else he's always ready, excessively ready, to talk. About that period – not a word.

He must think I'm some species of idiot, if he imagines I wouldn't notice a silence of that kind. In fact, I find the couple of years missing in his career just after the end of the war to be quite as much of a giveaway as the five years that preceded them. We know how much and what sort of employment the Nazis found in their camps and elsewhere for cooperative doctors. Subsequently he would have needed those two years to sink out of sight while the chase after war criminals was at its height. Then he could make his way back to Switzerland, and set himself up once again as the compassionate, wise, suave, cultivated healer and collector of jade trifles he now pretends to be.

I know, I know. It's all been put behind us. It was over before I was born. There have been other mass crimes before and since. True, also, that refugees like papa have always felt an unspoken, deep guilt not only towards those of their own people who didn't manage to get away, but also – horrible though it is to admit it – towards their persecutors. Towards all untouched bystanders and onlookers, too, if it comes to that. And their guilt has been passed on to the next generation. Me, for example. The squalor of what occurred! The unseemliness of it! The shame of having been involved, and in such a role, in so much utterly pointless misery and degradation! From which not a single improving moral can be drawn; out of which no prospects for a grander future for all mankind obligingly open before us . . . No wonder we all do our best to avoid thinking about the whole business.

But sometimes the effort is too great. Like now. Like when I think of Dr Wuchs. Of his pale, watery eyes. Of his soap-scented hands.

After Buchan had left me I may have fallen asleep, because of the evil injection he'd given me. But I did later manage to go for a walk in the woods. It was just as I had imagined it would be. Only I had left out something. The midges. There were lots of them about. Now I scratch, like a fool. I write and I scratch. I can hardly tell one spasm from the other. Which itch is which.

W riting and scratching, all the time spreading more widely the minute doses of poison just under my skin, and making the white mounds on it weep their single tears, it's natural that I should feel like tormenting Timothy. Why shouldn't he suffer too? Don't I suffer when I think of him? All the time!

So let me put him through a few of the conversations he had with Susie before and after she went to college. They were an unfailing source of torment to him, both when they occurred and in the endless, tedious repetition of memory.

How about this one? There he stands in the Sendin living room, in front of the case that contains Mr Sendin's trophies. In their shining convexities he discerns many small, worthless reflections of himself.

Now his belly appears to be swollen into a false pregnancy; then the top of his head aspires to a ridiculous point; next he finds his own double-barrelled nose pointed at him like an outmoded piece of artillery. Susie looks severely at his back, before she takes off her glasses, having seen enough.

'You're not a proper person to me,' she says. 'You're just a name I remember. Somebody from my childhood who's suddenly come back and won't go away again. I hardly remember anything about you.'

'I remember everything about you.'

'Was I nice?'

'No.'

'Was I nice to you?'

'No. Not at all.'

He has turned bravely to answer her. But without her glasses she can't see the expression on his face, which looks blurred and streaky to her, like the one unusable double-exposure from a roll of snapshots.

'Do you believe I've changed?'

'I don't know.'

Susie's enlarged, complex eyes stare thoughtfully at nothing in particular. 'I don't think I've changed,' she says. 'If I were you I really would go away and stay away.' She sighs, gets up from the couch, and says in a different tone of voice, 'I'll tell Laurence that you came to see him.'

'I came to see you.'

'That's not what you said at the door.'

'I was lying.'

'I know . . . I knew.'

She waits for him to go out. As he passes her it surprises him, even now, to see how much shorter she is than himself. At school they had been the same height. It seems wrong to him that they shouldn't be so still.

'I used to follow you when I saw you in the street. I couldn't understand why Laurence didn't invite me to your house. I thought it was because your parents were against me. Or because you were. I didn't know it was just Laurence himself who was keeping me away.'

'Perhaps he thought he was doing me a favour.'

'You're teasing me!'

'Am I? I suppose I must be. I don't know . . . How is Laurence? I never see him nowadays. Is he still driving his van around?'

'Yes.'

'What's his room like?'

'Just a room. Like mine.'

'So he drives his van, and you sit in your old shop . . . Honestly, I don't understand either of you. Haven't you got any ambition?'

Yes, he has got ambitions, Timothy tells her, speaking in a manner that is suddenly much more distant and yet more self-assured than before. He has many ambitions. He thinks about them all the time. Does she want to know what they are? Really? Very well. He's saving up bit by bit until he will have got enough money together to open a shop of his own. A jewellery shop. Perhaps antiques and pictures as well. The kind of shop he's working in now is the most miserable poor relation of the one he's going to have. (Still, what he's doing now is good practice. He's lucky to have the chance of it. She shouldn't look down on it so much.) He has become very interested in jewellery. In precious stones particularly. Obsessed by them. He reads up about them in books: on geology, crystallography, spectroscopy, handcrafts, history, thrillers. Books like that. He goes to the Geological Museum to look at specimens. He visits the galleries and the shops in the West End. He's even been . . . yes, he's even been . . . buying some stones; nothing very much; only what he can afford; what he needs for study.

'Well, that sounds like quite a good idea,' says Susie, surprised by his intensity, more impressed by the answer she has called forth than she had expected to be. 'You should be able to make a lot of money that way.'

Yes, he wants to make money. He wants to be able to afford the best of everything. But money isn't the point. The point is –

She prods into the abrupt silence that has fallen on him. 'Well?'

He has to learn from them. From the stones. Not just about them; anyone could do that. Learning from them is more difficult.

'What on earth do you mean?'

Being. Total being. What it is. Sustaining the greatest possible pressures in the smallest possible space. That's what he must learn. And more. The thing is –

Another silence. This time Timothy himself interrupts it. He begins to lecture her on the subject of crystals in general and gemstones in particular: their hardness on the Moh scale, their colour, their durability, the regularity and simplicity of their molecular structures, to which they owe so many of their other qualities. He talks of space lattices, angles of refraction, X-ray diffraction patterns, cleavage planes. Stones like these are the most perfect forms of matter we know, he tells her earnestly. It was through studying them that men began for the very first time to understand the internal structures of all solids. They are what nature would produce invariably, in every combination of elements, if only she were given the right temperatures and time and peace enough. That's how he sees it, anyway. It's obvious there are hierarchies of matter. Even as a kid he'd known that. Especially as a kid. These stones are the angelic orders of matter. They are god-like. That was why men had always been driven to look for them; dug for them in every corner of the globe; paid such prices for them; killed each other to get them; always, unconsciously, worshipped them. Quite rightly! Not enough!

Susie laughs. 'Timothy, you are mad.'

He denies it. One day she'll see for herself. He'll show her. The stones will show her. When they're working in the shop together, he and she. They'll be married, of course. They'll be living happily ever after. Until they die ... Unless a cure for dying has been found by then.

Susie laughs again. 'Oh, you're going to do that too.'

Well, he can't call that one of his ambitions; it's one of his hopes, rather. He tries to explain what he means. How it might be achieved. He mentions 'crystalline evolution', 'projected life', 'solid state sublimation, as with naphthalene', and several more topics of the same kind. Susie doesn't know that some of the

terms he uses have been invented *ad hoc*, on the spot.
Nor does Timothy. There must be a mistake somewhere, he concludes, simply and modestly. The substances of which we are composed don't die. Yet we
do. There must be a way of putting it right.

'Let me know if you ever find it.'

'Oh, I will, Susie. I'll do it for you.'

Susie beckons him to come closer to her. She studies him at close quarters, before pulling a little face.
'I can see into your future better than you can,' she
says. 'I have magical scientific powers that tell me
exactly what's going to happen to you. Do you want
to know? Do you dare to hear?'

'Of course, tell me, Susie.'

'One day somebody – I can't see who, but somebody – is going to come into your shop and try to buy
you. He'll say, "Well, if you dust him off and clean
him up a bit, you could almost take him to be a real
person, not a dummy at all." '

Now a silent conversation. They had some of those
too.

Susie sits next to Timothy. Her arm is against his.
He can feel the pressure of it as he stares ahead at the
immense lit-up pictures on the screen, or looks up at
the beam that projects them there, and sees how it
flicks, jumps, alternates in intensity from one side of
itself to the other, but never ceases to point its lessons
to the rows of watching heads beneath. His mouth
dry and his heart hammering at the liberty he is about
to take, assailed by a sudden, additional fear of under-
arm odour, he lifts his arm and stretches it out on the

140

back of the seat Susie occupies. He glances at her and she at him, in the half-light. He can make out her features and the dark shafts and round frames of her glasses. Her lips are dark too. Now that he's made his move, he doesn't know what to do with the hand at the end of his outstretched arm. It clutches the wooden back of her seat, then hangs over the end of it, then stands up at right angles from his wrist.

She doesn't come closer to him or move away from him. The beam of light above them goes on with its work, smoke rises through it, the pictures in front of them continue to change incessantly, voices boom, music starts and stops. Timothy's arm begins to ache. Desperately he wills Susie to snuggle up against him. She remains unmoved by his silent pleas and conjurations. In a fit of daring or anger he takes a firm hold of her bare upper arm. How soft it is between his fingers! How dry, how warm, what a tremulous fullness is contained, only just contained, within it!

But he is permitted to hold the weight of it for a moment only. Susie's hand comes up across her body, she gives his hand a rebuking tap, and puts it back on the wooden top of the seat.

A soliloquy, addressed in the middle of the night to an absent one:

'Bitch! Bitch! Bitch!'

Susie to Timothy, just after writing exams at the end of her first year in college, and just before going on a camping holiday in France with a fellow-student called Barry:

141

'You are sweet. You really shouldn't bother about me. I'm no good for you, Timothy. I'm sorry it has to be like this.'

From France she sent him a picture postcard of a village of white houses with red-tiled roofs clambering up the slope of a hill. The card said: 'The French are *awful*, but this place is just super. Love, Susie.'

'Why do you keep on and on and *on* at me? Do me a favour and find someone else, for God's sake!'

'There's no-one else. Not for me.'

'Why? Why not? What makes you say things like that?'

'There's never been anyone else. Sometimes when I look into your eyes I think I've died already. Don't laugh. Don't be cross. This isn't something I asked for. It happened. Years ago. It's given. Now I've got to find out what it's for. What it wants. Then I must obey. My only hope is to be obedient. Yours too.'

In spite of having asked for this declaration, Susie hasn't listened to it. She has one of her own to make.

'You want to persecute me, that's the real truth. You want to pay me out, I don't know why. I can see it. I'm not a fool. But you mustn't bluff yourself that I'm going to give in to you. I won't. I never will. I'll never belong to you. Never. Never.'

Enough of conversations for the moment. Instead, some observations.

Because she grew up to have an appetite for strong drink and strong sex, Susie believed herself to be passionate and impulsive by temperament. She was neither.

Because her calculations and her contrivances were all short-term, like her sight, she imagined she wasn't mean or devious. She was both.

She was vain too. Witness her preoccupation with her glasses. She wore them at the cinema and when she was reading or working, but never, if she could possibly help it, at other times. In the street she would take them out of her handbag and peer through them at the number of an approaching bus, then put them away hastily. She would rather ruin her eyes than ruin the effect they had on others. Few who looked into her eyes were inclined to blame her for this. Timothy was not among them. One long vacation she worked in a shop in order to earn enough money to buy a pair of contact lenses. When she put them in, they made her cry. She wept for weeks, stubbornly, blindly, angrily, hoping that the irritation they caused would go away. It did not. She went back to using her glasses.

She had no curiosity about the lives of others. This never prevented her from confidently passing opinions on all subjects. Especially on the relationship between men and women, on which topic she believed herself to be rapidly becoming an authority.

'You think you love me,' she told Timothy sternly, 'because you want to believe that you do. You've been told about love, so now you have to pretend to feel it.'

As if imparting to him a truth arrived at only after much daring and original thought, she said, 'If people didn't read books and go to the cinema, they wouldn't fall in love.'

She believed sex to be a good thing, of course. On the whole she was in favour of marriage too, provided you didn't think of it as the end of your right to have fun. Eventually, she supposed, everyone had to settle down; you couldn't live alone all your life, particularly if you wanted to have children. It stood to reason. But as for love!

'In a few years' time,' she instructed Timothy, 'you'll be wondering what on earth you ever saw in me.'

Timothy listened to her babble. He knew it to be babble. Sometimes it irritated him. Sometimes it amused him. Most often it made him feel sorry for her; it aroused his protective instincts. How little she knew! But he did not try to enlighten her. He let her talk. He watched out for glimpses of the crooked teeth he adored. Little words of ivory they were, that spoke to him in quite a different language from that of her tongue. Or he stared into the impenetrable mosaic of her eyes. The pattern within them appeared to him like a work of art he would one day be able to interpret, if only he was persistent enough.

She had so many ways of leading him on! All girls had them, it was true: soft ways, shining ways, swelling ways within their blouses. He had made a note of them. But Susie's were incomparable in their variety and power. Even her habit of going out with other men was just another example of her cunning.

Girls had to be like that. He had worked out why. From the blind seedling in the ground, splitting the cotyledon which fed it, to that which it so much resembled, the wet, tiny tip of a woman's sex, cur-

144

tained in the delicate folds of her own flesh – it was the same rapacity, the same greed for life and growth. Then death. That was all women were good for. He had seen as much for himself. He had read about it in his books. He had got additional information from Mrs Davis and other females, some of whom he had paid for their demonstrations. He was sure that when the time finally came for him and Susie to set up house together, she would be surprised at how much he had taught himself.

There would be other surprises in store for her, as well. He wasn't yet sure what they would be. He was waiting for instructions from the tiny lordly presences he had secreted in his room. They never ceased to shine in the darkness of their place of concealment. He added to their number whenever he could. Every day that passed he was nearer to finding out what they wanted of him.

'Mabel's very fond of you, Timothy. I know she is. She's told me so. You really must try to be kind to her. She's very sensitive. And she hasn't had much luck – with her family, or with men, or with anything, really. So you will try, won't you, Timothy? For my sake?'

Of course he'll try. Of course he did. Thus he acquired another good source of tormenting recollections: his encounters and conversations with Susie's large, sluggish friend from college. By and large he and Mabel disliked each other; they had little say to each other. But they had a fatal allegiance in common. They were both at the service of Susie.

So picture the two of them, Mabel and wonder-working, message-expecting Timothy, dancing up and down, up and down, while they look around for Susie in the crowded, noisy college dining hall, perfunctorily transformed into a pleasure palace by dangling strips of red crepe and coloured lanterns. Picture them out on a bench, surrounded by a litter of cardboard cups thrown down by other revellers. A damp smell rises from the muddy turf at their feet. Blasts of music sound in their ears from the hall behind them. Oblongs of light from its windows lie flat on the lawn, like playing cards put out in a game of patience. From Mabel not a word. None from Timothy either. When he puts his arm around her, she responds immediately by sliding a heavy thigh into contact with his; she turns her face, which is triangular in shape, towards him. The back of her head is flat, and she has a mass of blond curls attached to it in wig-like fashion. He imprints a kiss on her large, stationary mouth. Each of them retires to take a few cautious breaths. He puts a hand on her breast. Beneath the material of the party-dress she is wearing, her flesh feels like nothing special, a neutral substance. She sighs conscientiously, and he gloomily squeezes.

'At it again!'

Susie has crept up behind them. Her mouth is black, her eyes shine, she wears over her shoulders the jacket of the young man who is with her. The jacket is much too big for her, and she looks fetchingly waif-like in it. Her chilled companion in shirtsleeves would rather that he and she were elsewhere, doing something else, as they have been until a short time before.

146

But it pleases Susie to see her two ungainly admirers embracing. She would like to see them performing other tricks. Balancing balls on the ends of their noses. Bursting through hoops of coloured tissue paper. Walking on ropes suspended above the ground. Begging for crumbs.

Separately and together, they obliged. While Susie amused herself with Barry or Gary or Harry, Mabel and Timothy went to the pictures together. They walked across this or that park. They sat in coffee bars. On one of their outings to Hampstead Heath, Mabel announced to Timothy that Susie had told her that even if she liked him more she would never marry him, because he was a Jew. She could never marry a Jew.

'I'm not a Jew.'

Timothy denied his father. It took no effort. He had denied his mother for Susie's sake ages previously.

They were walking near Kenwood House. The white grass of winter was matted together with the new season's green; leaves were crumpled, soft, pale, still infantile in appearance; a dreamy sky mixed indiscriminately sun and cloud and its own blue vacancies of mind. Now close, now suddenly distant, the buildings of Highgate appeared at the end of oddly improbable chasms and absurd slopes, as if to make things easy for the weekend painters who had put up their easels at various points of vantage. Children rang among trees, and young men and women held hands and pressed the sides of their hips together as they emerged from secluded pathways. Mabel and Timothy walked in single file, always a few paces

147

apart.

'Susie says you're a Jew.'

'She doesn't want to marry me, anyway.'

But how much of a comfort was that to him? When he turned his head he could see how amused Mabel was at his reply. Though her mouth had not opened, it had at least broadened; the narrow blue slits of her eyes shone.

'Would you marry me, if I asked you to?'

'Ask me and see.'

'No, I won't.'

The sun came out strongly. Some trees at the top of a nearby slope acquired a wealth of metallic shadows. And at once began to lose them. The shadows faded, they lost their colour, they sank into the ground and disappeared entirely, like water. Gone. Timothy stared where they had been. The swiftness of the alternations seemed to have been put on display for him alone. What if it were all a dream – not the changing world, but his private plans to undo the necessities that kept it together? If it would never yield, never had, was as indifferent to his efforts and projects as the tree had been to its own shadows that had come and gone? Laurence was a petty thief. He was a fence. Mabel was ugly. Susie didn't care for him. None of it mattered in the least. That was the truth. There was no other.

He took Mabel to his room. He persuaded her to remove her clothes. Having sworn her to secrecy, he opened Susie's spectacle case. Inside it he kept the treasures he was collecting. Most of them were tiny stones he had torn from their mountings, including the very first from the ring Laurence had given him.

Now he disposed them in different places on Mabel's body: eyelids, breasts, palms of the hands, between her legs, on her tongue. She was quite willing to help him. He studied the stones in their new settings, like a diviner. Their gaze of different colours winked at him, but never wavered. Something in his head moved sharply sideways, leaving the room behind. At the same moment he felt a sickening vacancy balloon out between his heart and his left arm, preventing him from bringing his elbow down to his side.

Such signs were difficult to interpret. Nevertheless, he chose to regard them as encouraging. So, in a different manner, did Mabel.

Lie still, Timothy. No, don't move. Trust me. Don't be afraid. I won't harm you. Just lie quietly. You see, you must give the stillness a chance. Then it can grow like a light. Like a jewel. Then you'll be able to see me. You'll find me, at last.

Where?

Here! – here! – here! – in this car that's trying to start.

The car gurgles, hawks abruptly, begins to snore its way into the distance, interrupting itself only to gulp once, and then a second time, further downhill. Lying on his back, looking at the pattern of lights gliding swiftly across the ceiling, Timothy listens to the receding, diminishing drone. He doesn't know what room he is in, or whose loving voice has just been whispering to him, or what trees those are that bend and rustle outside his window. He wonders who is seated at a desk near the window, with his back towards him, and what are the lines that the stranger's hand is

149

making as it moves ceaselessly back and forth across a white, lamplit page.

Just as I thought. Young Buchan asked me about the writing I've been doing. Obviously, papa must have phoned up from London and spoken to them about it. (Taking a liberty, I call it, in the circumstances.) Buchan asked me, politely enough, if he could see some of my work. I said no. He asked me why not. I said: for personal reasons. He didn't pursue the matter. But I'm going to be very careful about not leaving any of my papers lying around, henceforth. Under lock and key they'll go. Definitely. And perhaps I'll try one of those old tricks like putting a hair across the pages, so that I'll be able to see at once if they have been tampered with by others.

So if you're reading this, Buchan, or Wuchs, or anyone else who's working for them, take it from me that I know already about your spying and your snooping. Not to speak of your breaking and entering. Laurence Sendin had more honour than any of you. And more skill.

And another message, while you're there. My subject is like a lump of matter on my tongue which I must swallow precisely because its taste and texture are so repulsive to me; like a nauseating smell I can't restrain myself from sniffing at until it penetrates my lungs and turns my guts; like the slack, stale body of a woman whom I fondle in order to show myself how free I am not to do it. In other words, my subject is obsession. Hence its rancid allure; its poisoned voluptuousness. Without these, how can obsession do its work? Sitting endlessly at this desk, unable to get away from it, remembering what I must, I speak whereof I know.

Also: obsession is motionless. It knows nothing of time. It knows only how to continue as before.

Powdered white, painted pink, dyed black, Elsie Brody terminated above in two thick horns of hair; below, in shiny shoes with delicate straps. Her English was atrocious. In the sitting room of her house in West Hampstead there were several photographs of the late Mr Brody. Overhead, noisy yet surreptitious footfalls and conversations indicated the presence of her many lodgers.

Gerhard married her. They were married in the Hampstead registry office, in the presence of the bride's daughters, sons-in-law, and Timothy. The ceremony was not a very moving one. Gerhard's demeanour was embarrassed but plucky. The new Mrs Fogel flared her capacious nostrils at everyone present, paying special attention to the registrar. She wore a many-layered green dress, and black stockings through which wide but eerie areas of whiteness could be discerned. Farewells were made outside, amid the indifferent din of traffic and the flashing of pedestrian beacons in the prematurely sallow evening air. The honeymoon was to be spent on the Italian Riviera; then the happy couple were to come back to Elsie's house.

So Gerhard returned to the continent for the first time since he had been chased out of it more than two decades before. He joined the early package tour crowds in Alassio. He sat in coaches that swayed and changed gears along the winding coastal road from San Remo in the west to Genoa in the east. He inspected the endless chain of seafront hotels and apartment blocks, most of them still empty at that time of year, all of them as disposable in appearance as cardboard boxes or egg-crates. He drank coffee in pavement cafes. He girded himself to perform his matrimonial duties. He began to get accustomed to his wife's little ways: her nibbling at a laxative chocolate after breakfast; the shedding of her corsets after lunch; the somnolent gargling in her throat after midnight. He wrote apologetic postcards to Timothy. He reluctantly answered his wife's questions about her newly acquired stepson.

She fished, she prowled, she wanted the lowdown. Was he a good boy? Yes. Who were his friends? Laurence Sendin. What were his ambitions? A shrug. Was he satisfied to spend the rest of his life in (excuse me) a second-hand shop? A shrug. What about girls? A shrug. A-levels? A shrug. Interests? Two shrugs.

His manner suggested to Elsie that he had something to conceal. But she was prepared to bide her time. Soon the honeymoon was over, and they returned to London, to find Timothy as dreamily unengaged as he had apparently been when they had left.

'So what's it like, papa, being a married man again?'

'Not too bad, it has advantages . . . It would be a fine thing if you were also to settle down one of these days, Timothy.'

'There's plenty of time.'

'Yes, there is, there is.'

There was always plenty of time. Especially in the shop. There, among the bits of china on tables and the large and small receptacles for a variety of contents on the floor, time seemed to be as much at a standstill as in the broken-down travelling clocks in glass and gilt cases that Gerhard was too often talked into buying. Many mornings passed without anyone crossing the threshold. Afternoons were usually a little busier. Occasionally Gerhard went out to visit the houses of people who had seen his advertisements in the local press, and had phoned to offer items of various kinds they wanted to get rid of. More often he sat at his bureau in the back room, sighing and staring at nothing, pushing up the flesh of one cheek with the hand that cupped his chin. In the shop, Timothy picked up some article or another at random and for the hundredth time ran the tips of his fingers over its surface, or brought it to his cheek, or scratched with his nail at its crevices and irregularities. Or he sat in a cane-backed rocking chair, forever riding to and fro,

155

forever getting nowhere. When a customer came in to browse among the bric-à-brac, he would put the book he was reading face down on the table next to him, ready to serve or just to watch. Often he looked up from his book into the empty shop simply in order to marvel that so much could be happening to others and (it seemed to him) with such speed – look, Maureen was dead, and Gerhard had already found a new wife; look, little Susie with whom he had been at school would soon be a teacher herself, like Polly Green – while he, Timothy, still waited to learn what was going to become of him.

But that was apparently how things had to be.

All his books told him that no flawless crystal had ever been grown in a hurry.

He continued to read books on scientific subjects that interested him. On antiques. On magic and mythology. On the embalming rites of the ancient Egyptians. Popular guides to philosophy and the wisdom of the east. He made many notes on pieces of paper of particular words and phrases he had come across in his reading. Diagrams, too. Graphs. Equations. Models of molecular structures. Sometimes he designed new ones, of his own imagining.

He knew and did not know that everything he read was eventually to fuse into a single gem in his mind; that the symmetries enclosing him right at the end were to be without flaw or occlusion; that the whole world would by then have become his perfect prison.

I mean, prism.

There were a few visitors to the shop with whom Timothy carried on a trade Gerhard knew nothing about. It was in order to be able to meet them more easily that he had come into the shop, in the first place. Gerhard did not know that either. The most assiduous of these confidential customers was a man who called himself Mr Farquarson. Neatly dressed and sweetly scented, he looked youthful and cocky with his hat on; when he took it off, revealing his bald cranium, he became the rotund uncle Timothy had never had. Timothy admired (and imitated) his sensitive manner of holding the items that were offered to him, as well as the lopsided unicorn or cyclops he turned himself into when he screwed his jeweller's optic into his eye. He paid for what he wanted from a roll of notes warmed and wadded together by the pressure of his plump buttock upon his back trouser pocket. Then he left without saying where he was going or when he would be returning. It was a most satisfactory relationship.

Laurence spent the money that came his way as a result of these transactions on clothes, girls, and gambling. Mad Timothy was more prudent. He continued to save up his money for the shop he intended to establish one day, and to take care of with the help of Susie. He was also carefully adding from time to time to his own collection of jewels, which was still small enough to be kept inside her spectacle case. Almost every night he opened the little case, looking with ever-renewed relish at its blue velvet lining and the tiny, oval strip of cardboard pasted against the inner lid, on which Susie's name appeared in her schoolgirl hand. Then he took the stones out one by one, carefully unwrapping them from the little twists of tissue paper in which they were folded.

Living pearls. Flat-bottomed opals, within which shifting grains of many indefinable colours never ceased trying to heap themselves over a vein of alabaster, that was itself in perpetual undulation. An aquamarine, cut as if directly from sunlight seen through water, looking up. A sapphire even bluer than the aquamarine. Grape-bloom amethysts. Three round garnets trembling like drops of blood just about to fall. Diamonds containing fires that blazed up demoniacally when they were provoked, and then swallowed their anger and merriment and lay down discreetly, as colourless as gin. A large, oval moonstone, transparent at first glance, around whose edges sly metallic gleams – of lead, silver, steel, copper, gold – were always chasing and replacing each other in tireless, eternal succession.

Each was its own world: complete, inviolable, different from every other, as full of change and drama as it was of an unalterable stillness. He never tired of examining them, either with the naked eye or under his glass. He played games with them. He arranged them in patterns on his table. He compared them with pictures of stones in his books. He had his own dream-names and dream-descriptions of them, which he whispered aloud to them sometimes, and which he changed as the fancy took him, knowing that they would always recognise their new appellations. He knew their scientific names too, and their chemical formulae; the conditions under which they were formed, and the matrices in which they were found; the subtly different rate at which they acquired heat from his fingers and gave it back. He knew more. He knew that substances so hard, so heavy, so immaculately ordered in their innermost structures, were God's purest thoughts.

He waited anxiously upon them. They kept him waiting.

Even when he learned about Susie's latest lover and whispered the news to them, they counselled one thing only. Patience. Patience. Patience. They seemed to forget that he was still human.

Of course, Susie had had men friends before. But the one she started an affair with during her last term at college was different. Mabel said so. Susie said so. Timothy saw it for himself. Again and again he saw it. He went to great trouble to see it.

They used to meet, Susie and her lover, in the Embankment Gardens, along with all the other office adulterers – older men, and girls in secretarial skirts and twinsets – who snatch their chance at one another's company between the end of the day's work and the departure of their homebound trains. On summer evenings many couples make their rendezvous there. Immediately above them, in almost Babylonian fashion, hang enormous buildings, stone staircases, roads on terraces; far below, at the bottom of the defile, under the steel coffers of a railway bridge from which thunders and groans can now and then be heard, the entrance to Charing Cross tube station is marked by a squalid collection of booths, barrows, and hot-dog stalls. It's in that direction they eventually have to go, after the talk between them, the kisses, the intent staring into the tiny confines of each other's eyes: the men to their wives and mortgaged homes in the suburbs; the girls to anxious parents or to flats they share with others like themselves. The sun still shines on buildings on the far side of the river, as if upon another country; the river itself is a running red, an oily black, on which bridges and anchored barges slide effortlessly against the current in order to remain where they are.

Leaves opened like the hands of statues, larger than life; the sky withdrew to its summer altitudes; the evenings grew longer, deeper, more commodious altogether. Timothy hid behind trees. He sat on little metal chairs with his coat collar turned up. He leaned over the parapets of terraces, holding a newspaper in front of his face. Sometimes he saw Susie and her friend sit together for a few minutes only before they parted; sometimes they went off arm in arm, and disappeared in the traffic of the Strand, and Timothy would assume they were going to spend the night together.

Watching them go, he pretended that he was already married to Susie; he was her injured husband spying on her betrayal of him. On other occasions he would be more modest; he would tell himself that he was merely the private detective hired by Susie's husband (himself) to present a report on her movements.

Either way, he went back home and prepared his bachelor dinner. While he ate it he imagined Susie coming in, with her lies about where she had been ready on her lips. He pretended to be taken in by her tales, and smiled, and offered her food. When she sat down opposite him, he quietly told her where he had been and what he had seen. She grew pale, she burst into tears over her plate, she confessed, she said that she loved the other man so much it was impossible for her to carry on as before.

He murdered her. Then he forgave her and set her free. She asked his pardon and swore on the Bible she would never see the other man again. They agreed to begin all over again, living like brother and sister.

He wiped her out by the power of projected thought, limb by limb, organ by organ, saving her consciousness for the last, so she would know to the end what was being done to her. She jeered at his projected thoughts, packed her bags, and walked out, while he watched her impotently; as she crossed the threshold he fell down in a swoon, with his heart's blood bursting out of his nose and mouth. She didn't look back at him, let alone call an ambulance.

He explained to her his multi-eye device, which enabled him to see whatever she did, wherever she went, at all times of day and night.

He wheeled out before her his space-time transfuser, which enabled him to bring her bewildered, trembling lover before him for punishment, at that very moment.

He threw the switch of his cryogenic encapsulator, which imprisoned Susie and her lover in an unmeltable block of ice, in which they were held fast forever, gazing at the onlookers who gazed at them, like two characters in a modern version of the *Inferno*.

He bestowed upon them both the vast wealth these inventions had brought him, so that they could set up house together. He became their dear, valued bachelor friend, godfather to all their children.

He cut out her lying tongue with laser beams and sent it in a jiffy-bag to her lover.

He transformed them both, with a wave of his hand, into two imbecile mannequins of wax and plaster, standing in absurd attitudes in the middle of his room, as though in a shop window. He used the skills he had acquired in The Sewing Basket to drape them in cloths of all kinds, and in costumes from different historical periods.

The variations of the game were endless.

But Susie didn't come through his door.

The summer continued to advance. The sound of transistors was heard in surburban gardens. Office workers sunned themselves in open spaces during lunch hours. Hopeful painters hung out their pictures against railings in Hampstead and Piccadilly. Roads were blocked with traffic every weekend. Girls applied deodorants more conscientiously than before to their shaven armpits. Roadmending gangs stripped themselves to the waist, revealing red necks, arms gauntleted in red, and candle-white torsos inscribed with savage tattoos. Lettuces dropped in price. The bare, uncovered legs of babies lying in their prams were cool to the touch. The death rate continued to decline from its mid-winter peak. A host of colleges closed their doors. Mabel left London for her home in Suffolk. Susie no longer came to the Embankment Gardens.

Only Timothy still haunted the place, out of habit. He watched the other people there, pretending to himself that this couple or that were really Susie and her lover.

What had actually happened was that Susie had been having it off with this man who worked for an oil company in town. Quite an old guy really: a married man, with a couple of kids. Now he'd put Susie up the spout. But he didn't want to know her troubles. He'd taken off. He'd already had himself transferred to Algeria or Kuwait or somewhere, one of those oily places.

Excited by his news, not at all displeased at Susie's misfortunes, Laurence talked busily. He'd heard about it from his mother. She was pretty sick about it. She was still trying to treat it like a big secret. But he didn't know how much longer it could remain one. The thing was, the real surprise was, that Susie had said she wanted to keep her little mistake. Her big mistake. She wouldn't hear of trying for an abortion, or of having the kid adopted when it arrived.

Timothy brought his rocking chair to a halt. 'Then she'll want help.'

'You bet she will.'

Laurence continued to talk. Timothy again began to rock himself backwards and forwards. The shop was empty but for the two of them, and for its silent litter that had been bought and sold and used many times over. Timothy was no longer listening. It was easy to pay no attention to Laurence. He knew nothing. He'd never been told about Timothy's attachment to his sister, and he was incapable of guessing it for himself. It had never occurred to him that Timothy might have cultivated his friendship for Susie's sake. He knew nothing about Timothy's collection of precious stones. His ignorance and

163

shallowness were altogether disgusting.

But enough! He'd been useful once; now he was just a nuisance.

Timothy rocked his chair faster. He had just thought of a way of expressing his changed attitude towards Laurence. It was quite simple. This was no occasion for the exercise of special powers. Laurence wasn't worthy of them. He deserved to live in a world stripped of alternatives.

Some days later Mrs Sendin received an anonymous letter. It said: 'Your daughter is a disgrace to a respectable neighbourhood. We know all about her. We know who she takes after too. It's a wonder that you dare to show your face in the streets.'

The signs have been getting clearer and clearer: my time here is definitely running out. The latest warning (if that's the word) was delivered earlier today. I found a stranger in possession of my room; not merely of my room, but of my bed. He resembled Mr Farquarson, but I can't believe it really was him. He was wearing striped pyjamas and down-at-heel slippers. One of his slippers was more off than on, and his clean, yellowish foot was exposed. He didn't seem at all taken aback to see me. In fact, he didn't move until I went to the bed and pulled him up by the arm. Then he got to his feet at once, in a perfectly submissive manner. His lips were round and colourless; I had the impression that within them I could actually make out their separate, plump, transparent inner cells, like those inside a slice of orange. The thought of it was somehow more sickening than the sight itself. My repulsion made me tighten my grip on his shoulder. He worked the loose slipper on to his foot. I led him to the door, pushed him out firmly, and slammed it shut.

But he'll be back. I'm sure of it.

A creeping disorder seems to be overtaking the whole place: a sinister slovenliness. The organisation's simply running down. You can see it everywhere. If you don't make up your bed it simply remains unmade. People walk about in pyjamas and dressing gowns at all hours of the day. The noise in the dining room is intolerable. The waiters splash your portions into your plate or on to your lap indiscriminately. The food is disgusting. Newspapers and empty cigarette packets lie about on the floors; plastic cups stand in their own sticky rings on every table top; no-one bothers to clear them away or to wipe off the marks. The linoleum in the corridors is full of holes. For the money they must be charging, it's a disgrace. And they're packing in more and more people all the time, without any consideration for those of us who are already here.

When I complained about it all to Marnie she answered me sharply, and in a peculiar way. 'What do you expect?' she said. 'Why should you be treated differently from the rest of us?'

I explained that I *was* speaking for all of us, precisely; not just for myself. But I could see she wasn't attending. She was moving her head about distractedly, pop-eyes much in evidence, as if waiting for somebody to come in at any moment to claim her.

Nobody did. The thought of exploring that intricate bridgework of hers with my tongue no longer has the faintest appeal. She is looking very poorly; her skin is lifeless and has become coarser in texture; dry flakes of stuff adhere to the corners of her lips.

Also, another reason why I know I haven't much time left here: I don't seem to be remembering things as vividly as I used to. I mean, the things I care about. That I really want to remember. Not Marnie. I can see her clearly enough. And that loony in my room this morning, pathetic creature. And Wuchs. (He hasn't been around for days. The crook.) No problem with them. But papa's face? A blank. Except for the thought of an anxious frown. Maureen? Gone. And that's not a loss I can get over so easily.

How idiotic it is, I now realise, to hanker after vulgarly supernatural powers of transformation, when the powers we have can perform such marvels for us, if only we allow them to. The power of love! Of memory! Of imagination! To be a boy walking home with his mother, centuries ago, to a little house halfway up a huddled terrace, where a clerkly jobbing painter waits patiently in his upstairs studio. . . What could be more precious and unassailable than such a memory? How can I not have understood until now that to want more is in the end to have less? And less. Until one has nothing at all: neither the present nor the past.

But I'm not going to go until I've finished my task. I don't care what they do to encourage me to leave. Or where they want me to go afterwards. I've got some important matters to settle while I'm here. I think.

He offered Susie everything he had. Himself. His unused and undefined powers, whose nature would soon be made clear to all. His jewels. The feats he had performed in his childhood. His shop.

She stood up from the bed, on which she'd been sitting since coming into the room. He took her hands in his. She pulled them away. She said, 'I knew it would be a waste of time coming here. You're crazy. You're getting worse all the time. I only came because I felt sorry for you. If you think that just because I'm in trouble I'd – '

Then she shouted: 'Don't touch me! I don't want you near me. You should see what you look like. Your face – your lips – '

She shuddered. At that moment it occurred to

Timothy that time itself was a simple crystal. If you looked at time with the right instruments, as he had just been compelled to, if you passed through it rays of the right wave-length, which would produce a scatter pattern open to correct interpretation, you could perceive that its structural units repeated themselves in endless, identical array through all eternity.

The baby inside Susie was proof of it. That baby had always been inside her, and inside that baby once again was the baby she herself had once been.

Therefore she had to scream. Then she would become Maureen, and the crystalline simultaneity of time would be made fully manifest. He would become Gerhard, the father of another man's child (himself), as he had always been. There were no accidents in the world; no screams without causes or consequences.

Therefore she had to scream.

She would do it shortly. It would signify her re-entry into re-eternity. There were no other words for what was to happen. At least, no other words he could think of.

First, however, he had to change his face. It was not difficult. Immediately he had done it, he saw the beginning of the scream rise up silently in her green/black/chipped eyes (behind glass, like trophies). It was a remarkable phenomenon. He had never seen such a look in her eyes before. This pleased him. It confirmed his belief that great changes were upon them both. He felt within him an intolerably light, delicate pang; not even the flutter of the finest scrap of cellophane through the air could be compared with its passage through him. And it gleamed as it went! It destroyed him, as he had been. He was made over. He became another consciousness.

All this, mind you, before so much as a single scream had been uttered by anyone. While she was still groping in the wardrobe for her raincoat, which had been hung up there when she had first come into the room. He said to her, and his voice surprised him by its similarity to that of the unresolved, supplicant Timothy of a few minutes before, 'As a matter of fact, it's too late.'

'How? What do you mean?'

Her coat was over her arm. He tried to take it from her. She wouldn't let him do it. Yet for a moment it seemed that they were as they had been when she'd been sitting on the bed, telling him of her plans (in which he had played no part). Calm. Tense. Strangers to one another. Exchanging banal remarks. Then let her hear more of them!

'Or it's too early. It makes no difference. It's all one. A simple substance.'

She turned to the door, with a gesture of anger or disgust.

He called her back. 'Susie.'

This time she screamed. It was beautiful. Just when she had forgotten the fear that had sprung into her eyes, and he had remembered the noise he still had to hear from her – just then, she opened her mouth, she displayed her crooked, Susie teeth, and moving tongue. It was quite a loud noise but it didn't last long. He clapped his hand across her mouth. He led her back to the bed. He had a lot to tell her. When he ran out of words he would learn what was to happen next.

Actually, Timothy had had an indication earlier that day, in the shop, that important developments were at hand.

It began with a conversation between him and Elsie. In the course of it she slyly revealed that she knew all about the habit he had had as a little boy of 'changing into different things'. And still had, perhaps, as a man?

At that point Gerhard, who had gone into his back room while they were talking, appeared at the door, a look of consternation on his face. Elsie was not deterred. Her eyes flashing with the concupiscence of curiosity, her nostrils dilating, she asked Timothy to show her what he used to do, so that she could see the trick for herself. Then she could decide whether or not he needed to go to 'a Psychiater'

Without effort, without practice, without warning, Timothy obliged her. He turned himself into the links of the necklace hanging around her neck. They were made out of some hollow, shiny, composite material; they had the diameter of macaroni, more or less, and the colours of neon. The lowest of the links were disposed comfortably on the slope of Elsie's well-trussed bosom. Timothy lay there too, in them, part of them, conscious not only of the sudden transformation he had just undergone, and of the stiffly breathing support beneath him, but also of further powers he was free to exercise if he so wished. For instance, he didn't have to remain his present size; the size that had, so to speak, been given to him. He could make himself smaller if he wanted to.

He did so. And again. The substance of himself

172

began to bite into Elsie's scented, powdered neck. He contracted himself yet further; he couldn't go back; he had to do just this, nothing else; Elsie would never witness a better demonstration of what his tricks were like. Tighter and tighter he became, smaller and smaller, in an unprecedented orgy of density, until he shattered with a loud report into a hundred pieces. The necklace went flying like shrapnel all over the shop. He found that he was clutching a few links of it in his hand. Elsie was sobbing over a sideboard a few feet to the left of him, and Gerhard was riding on his back, beating his fists against his head.

Timothy shook him off quite easily. Later he was to remember a book flying briefly through the air, its pages labouring like white wings. Also further shouts, sounds of breakage, and silence. Then he was in a phone booth, talking to Susie. She listened to him. She obeyed his orders. She walked into his room.

Little Susie, big Susie, his own Susie, he saw her at last within walls that had contained her image innumerable times, but never once her body. The fact that she was in the room just as the baby was inside her body offered him yet another illustration of the crystalline structure of time. Each fragment of the lattice was bound to be an exact facsimile of every other, and of the whole as well.

He remembered to tell Susie the story of Elsie's visit to the shop, and of how successfully he had performed his trick for her. He told her also about the evenings he had spent spying on her and her lover in the Embankment Gardens, and about how he had waited for her to come to his room afterwards, night after night. He spoke to her of the dislike and gratitude he felt towards Mabel, whom he called Maybe because he had decided that the name suited her. He recalled glimpses he had had of Susie in the street, when he and she had been attending different schools, years before. He told her about his memories of the days they had spent together in the same class at primary school. He reminded her of his first sight of her in the park, on the swings. He called her by some of the secret names he had never dared to utter before, not even to himself. Names like Susie-stone, Susie-sky, Susie-sand.

She made no reply. She had already been his Susie-scream. Now she was his Susie-silence. His Susie-stillness, too.

He could remember vaguely that there had been some difficulty to overcome before she had earned these new names. There had even been a knock on the door, from one of the other lodgers who lived down the corridor, and who had apparently been disturbed by what he called 'all that racket'. Timothy had assured him through the closed door that there would be no more noise. And he had kept his word, though he had still had some work to do at that point – cleaning, straightening, wiping, rearranging. Work of that kind. But he had been able to do it all very quietly.

Now he listened carefully to her silence. He examined her stillness.

It was amazing. There was no sound to be heard in the room but that of his own whispering voice. Once or twice he had to sing or hum softly. The rest of

London had closed all its doors and mouths. Its northern hills, whose weight he had felt so often upon his back, like a hump, crushing the life and breath out of him, had become as insubstantial as shells, patterned haphazardly with patches of light and darkness. The only heavy thing left in the whole world was his own hand, lying on Susie's motionless thigh. The night was a slow wave; he would have drifted away entirely on it, like a stamp peeled from damp paper, had he not been anchored by that hand of his. Even his voice drifted from him in the end, like the rest, taking with it all its words.

Though he lacked or needed nothing, sleep came as a profound yearning. He did not feel the yearning; it felt him. It stood beyond his awareness, and reached towards him longingly. It wanted him. It needed him. What it yearned for was to be him, who was the only form it could ever assume.

Timothy dreamed (or dreamed he was dreaming) that he and his wife, Susie Fogel-Truter, returned to London, to their flat in Wimpole Street. Among the doctors. From the tall windows of their drawing room they could see cars depositing patients of every age before shining black doors with highly polished brass bells and knockers attached to them. There were hundreds of Britain's leading specialists, all at the peak of their earning power, for blocks around. Thousands of patients came to visit them every day. Susie was excited by the thought of so much money and reputation being made out of suffering and death. It seemed appropriate to her, somehow.

Her own health was excellent; so was Timothy's. They lived there simply because they liked the neighbourhood. On one side was Regent's Park, the foliage of its trees and beds of flowers constantly altering with the season, while the elaborate stucco capitals and columns of the Nash terraces remained in perpetual leaf. On the other side was the West End. The noise of traffic was a problem; but where, Susie would ask rhetorically, in a manner which she was consciously cultivating to go with her new flat, was one free of it nowadays?

Her visitors included, at long intervals set sternly by Susie herself, her mother and her red-faced father, who winked and jerked his head in Timothy's direction when he came in, to show how much at ease he was, and left with a curious, sour shrug of his shoulders each time. They had their friends in more often: Vuskovic, the painter; Sanders, the sculptor; Gaffen, the philosopher; Beiwort, the art historian; Teddy Gristwold, the novelist, and his silky, sulky wife. Susie herself was doing a course at the Van Niekerk Institute of Fine Arts; and Timothy had been apprenticed to a dealer in Hatton Gardens. When Susie wanted to belittle him – when she was in the arms of Vuskovic for example – she would call Timothy 'the jeweller' or 'the watchmaker'. When she was feeling more kindly disposed to him she would say (with just a shade of embarrassment) that her husband was in precious stones.

Every weekday morning she saw him off with a kiss. He wore a business suit and carried a brief case. He walked to his office, in good weather and bad, for the exercise. His office was on the second floor of a building fronted with cheese-coloured marble; it contained little but a couple of desks, a safe embedded in the wall, and trimly bearded, blue-eyed Mr Goldstein, the gentleman from whom Timothy was learning his trade. The plan was that he would retire, suitably recompensed, within a year or two, when Timothy had learned all he could from him and was ready to take over the business.

Inevitably, time hung heavily on Susie's hands, in spite of her studies. So she turned for entertainment to the hairy Vuskovic, whose pictures were much admired by critics and sought after by collectors, and whose fingers were always green and black with the traces of oil paint he could never scrub from them. Vuskovic ate copiously, as if with the deliberate intention of extending even further the large belly he already had. He made love in much the same style, with a self-absorbed greed and persistence that Susie took to be a tribute to the plump, high-breasted figure she proffered to him. They embraced in his studio, on a disordered bed, under a window through which the prone Susie saw the light of the sky gleaming and waning in the random English manner – often dim at noon, brightest in the late afternoons, as the comings and goings of unseen clouds determined. Vuskovic laboured and floundered over her, but was never at a loss. Then she returned to the severe, flat-fronted house in Wimpole Street, whose only vestige of expression was given to it by the fan-like arrangement of bricks above each window: a settled frown of rebuke that Susie never felt to be directed against herself.

She went shopping. Timothy often accompanied

her. They bought Chesterfield cabinets, lion-footed, gilded chairs, Turkish rugs, Georgian silver and glass, damask linens, a brocade to cover their couch. They bought a giant, incongruous Vuskovic to hang on their wall: a green and scarlet affair of thick scrawls and portentous blobs, entitled Proproetides One. Timothy paid for the painting, and paid also for the silk scarves, coloured shirts, and gold signet rings with which Susie decorated her lover. He wore his finery whenever he came to dinner or for drinks at the flat.

The story could have gone on longer, Timothy felt: it was so interesting: so painful and yet at the same time reassuring. It presented a way of life, after all. Professional help of the very best kind was always near at hand in it. But then it flew loose. It became mixed up with a crowd of strangers and some scaffolding erected in a public square for a mysterious purpose. It was all in a book he was reading. A young, fair-haired man, elegantly dressed, turned in the entrance to the book, which had become a building too; he was holding in his hand a fragile glass vessel of much value, with a tapering stopper in its neck. He said, 'All right, then. I'm a liar.' Timothy opened his eyes with a feeling of great sadness. He was not surprised to find Susie lying on the bed beside him, on her back, just as he had left her.

Among all his other cares, Timothy didn't forget some details that had to be attended to.

Speaking just above a whisper, he told the sleepy police sergeant on the other end of the wire that he had an important tip-off for him. A watch should be put on a house at such-and-such an address in Finchley North. It was going to be raided within the next few days by a housebreaker who had been giving them a lot of trouble lately. His name was Laurence Sendin, and he lived at . . .

Timothy did not leave his own name and address with the policeman. He put the phone down and crept as quietly as he could back to his own room. There he wrote another anonymous postcard to Mrs Sendin, asking her which one of her two children she was more proud of: her son the thief, or her daughter the whore.

Then he returned to the bed, and composed himself to think the thoughts of God.

Now it was morning. Timothy sat in an underground train. To the best of his knowledge he was going to Susie's flat to pack her clothes. Susie could not go herself, for obvious reasons. The train swayed, roared, bounded, it shook bunches of cables threateningly at him through the glass of its windows. The people sitting in the seats opposite him, their bodies shaking to the train's rhythms, looked even more tired than they would going home from work that afternoon: puffier, paler, more dejected. Timothy watched them closely. He saw this man's eyes flicker from point to point along the tunnel through which they were all travelling. He saw another man's hand come up to scratch his cheek. He used two fingers. A woman's tongue appeared between her painted lips, it licked them, and disappeared. A fourth passenger breathed in acrid smoke and blew it out in a grey funnel that existed for as long as the exhalation that produced it. Looking at them, Timothy knew that each person there, each centre of consciousness, each envelope of selfhood, was in itself no more than a single organ of perception: the mobile, complicated feeler of some larger being, who was continually collating and making sense out of the reports they all sent back.

The purpose of it was plain. If the thoughts of God were matter, as Timothy knew them to be, it was clear whose spies the passengers were. Himself included.

The devil's.

So were trees, snakes, moss, bacteria, roses: everything that lived and ingested and reproduced. As sources of intelligence, however, none of the other forms of life could begin to compare in efficiency with people. Once the devil wanted to know what it was like to sit in a London tube train at that hour of the morning, the train rocking your body, its roar in your ears, a green coat on your shoulders and pointed brown shoes on your feet, your lips damp from a recent licking, staring at Timothy Fogel-Truter, who stares back at you – then he had no alternative but to employ that woman, exactly as she was. Of course her reports bored him intolerably as they came in, over and over again. Everything bored him. But that only made him more malign and inventive yet, determined to use more and more of God's innocent, insensible molecules for purposes ulterior to themselves. He made eyes scurry this way and that; fingers reach into a nostril or ear and scratch there; a spine rise delicately and straighten to let pass a bubble of gas. Even that, after so much time had passed, he still wanted to know! Who wasn't guilty of telling him? Telling him everything?

But there was a difference between Timothy Fogel-Truter and the others.

Only then did he remember what he had accomplished. In the swaying train he took the spectacle case that had once been Susie's out of his pocket. He opened it.

There they were: all the aspects of Susie that had most baffled and humiliated him, everything that was intrinsic to her, transformed at last into the thoughts of God.

The rest of her, which lay on the bed where he had left it, staring up at the ceiling it could no longer see, with or without its glasses – that too he honoured. It too had been redeemed from the illness of life. Withdrawn from the corruption of consciousness. Liberated from servitude. But not even in his farthest, spinning world could God produce substances which were more wholly themselves than those which Timothy held in his hand. This time they had not come into being in the inconceivable heat and pressure of volcanic pipes bursting out of the centre of the earth; but in a man's mind.

His. His own. Unaided. He had put his head against Susie's, his hands against hers, his stomach against hers, his legs and feet against hers. No clothes between them. No light to distract them. No words to mislead them. She offered no resistance. He summoned himself together to become a will or intention so pure he would be desireless, completely at rest within its grasp. His task was to give birth to what he had never conceived; suffer rendings and joinings that were not within him and added nothing to him; endure the recollection of what didn't exist. It was easy. It was quick. He had been so well prepared for it, over so many years. He was breathed in and exhaled by pain, just once. He flowed like an electric liquid through blind velvet channels; both they and he remained perfectly dry. There were some commonplace bumps and thumps, like those of books being dropped from a table. He wanted to sneeze, and could not. Time uncoiled itself within his skull and stretched out into the remotest distance. Space contracted into a single moment, a blink, that was gone. Someone cried, not him, not Susie, for an incalculable loss.

What had he done? What would he find when he opened his eyes?

He looked into his hand. God's most lustrous thoughts shone in it. He recognised them at once. Susie's malice, a green zircon. Her lust, an eight-sided ruby. Her intellect, cloudy topaz. Her pregnancy: a citrine within which was occluded another complete, perfect crystal of citrine. Her pride, a small diamond. Her fear, a lump of yellow talc. Her fate, rock salt.

No wonder he had dreamed of the Proproetides, transformed into stone for their shamelessness! He had them in his hand. They were his, entirely his, never to be taken from him. No-one could say now that he hadn't fulfilled the promise of his childhood.

But Susie didn't need her clothes any more. It had been absurd for him to suppose so. It wasn't for that purpose that he had got into the train. Or that it was running underground. Rather, it was taking him to the source of all God's thoughts, the place where they all came from. It would show him more of them. Imagine, all the passengers on the train struck into stone or iron! Or, even better, turned into giant crystals; transported back to God in a form which he himself found so difficult to think of. Waiting on the platform, standing forever on escalators that no longer moved, scattered thickly on pavements, gleaming behind the wheels of cars . . . It was almost too much to hope for. Certainly too much for one man to accomplish.

Later Timothy sat on a bench in a park. Clouds were gathering overhead. It was going to rain. Trees made weak, placatory gestures; they consulted with one another about what to do next, and then went on exactly as before, scraping and bowing effusively before every current of air. Two girls chased tennis balls about on an asphalted court, behind wire netting. The park keeper sat in the doorway of his pungently tea and tobacco-scented hut, watching the smoke from his pipe being snatched away from him at intervals by the breeze. Small, dark, fast-moving blobs of traffic made noises in the distance, and flashed from time to time. To all these movements were added those of Timothy's lips opening and closing rapidly, hanging apart, striking against one another with renewed vigour.

He was working out his plans for the future. Some children came to watch him. They stood on a path a few yards away, behind tiny railings like intersecting semi-circles of wire embedded into the ground. A group of workmen walking by stared, nudged each other, and grinned.

Let them.

The plan he worked out was this. He would sell his stones, all his stones, including the latest he had acquired, which were the finest of the lot. With the proceeds he would set up his father and himself in a business of the kind he had always dreamed about. Susie wouldn't be able to help him in it, as he had always hoped she would. But that was no reason for him to abandon the rest of his ambitions. No reason at all. He was surprised at how little he cared about her now. There were plenty of other women about. He might quite easily find someone to take her place. You never could tell.

But first he had to have a holiday. The strain he had been through, the efforts he had just made, had left him feeling utterly depleted. Never before in his life had he felt so tired. Even his sight was affected by his exhaustion. The children in front of him were more like fairground cut-outs than people; the heads of the workmen who had passed by had actually appeared to him to be transparent. They still did. He looked through them to small, sharp images hanging at eye-level under the trees. Nonsensical images, that had nothing to do with him or with each other: the distillation tower of a refinery, an oversized plastic butterfly, a woman walking about in her kitchen.

How he needed rest! Treatment too . . . The thought of placing himself in skilled hands gave him a great feeling of relief, as if he had been striving towards it for many months, even years perhaps. What was more, he could afford to do it now. He could permit

184

himself a few luxuries. He simply had to arrange his affairs (and his father's), and then he could be off. Where to? He considered for a moment only. Where did people like himself, people with money to spend and hence a free choice in the matter – where did they go for their health? Where were the most famous clinics in Europe to be found? The most advanced treatments for fatigue and nervous disorders? Where could one be sure of clean air, clean water, mountain views, good food . . .?

There was only one place.

He got up from the bench.

The people he dealt with were most understanding. They couldn't have been more helpful. They smiled, they bowed, they sent a special car for him, they helped him into it, they drove to where he told them to, they helped him out at the other end, they ushered him into quite another world.

Such fine prospects, so much attention to his needs, so handsome a city to visit if he chose, such leisure and freedom and privacy, such blue skies above and ample walks below – after a few hours it seemed to Timothy that he had been there for days. After a day, for many weeks. It was all exactly as he wished it to be. The doctor who was treating him turned out to be a bit of a charlatan, unfortunately; otherwise he had no complaints. The change alone was of absolutely immeasurable value to him.

The cups are lined in rows on a trolley next to the tea urn. Everyone has to fill his cup under the dribbling tap; then help himself to sugar and to milk from a tin bowl and jug. Some people drink their tea standing by the urn; others take it to their little cubicles off the main corridor, or go to the communal area right at the end of the building. There are a few battered armchairs in that corner, some pictures pinned on the wall, a couple of tables at which we have our meals. This morning one of the men who had just filled his cup with tea and milk proceeded very gravely and slowly to pour it all over the floor, as if he were watering a bed of flowers. No-one took the slightest notice of him. The mess remained on the linoleum for hours. People trailed their slippers and the cuffs of their pyjama trousers in and out of it. It wasn't until lunchtime that it was wiped up.

Most people wear nothing but pyjamas and dressing gowns day in and day out. If you want to go outside for a walk, however, you have to change into your clothes. That's one of the rules they're most strict about. Not that there's much to see or to do when you do go out. Just asphalt paths and roads winding about among a host of identical brick buildings: rather gaunt, barrack-like affairs of brick, three or four storeys high. Each of them has an iron fire-escape clapped to its side, like a fearsome orthopaedic appliance. Some of the buildings are for men, others for women. There are lawns and flower beds here and there, a number of pre-fabricated huts, and batteries of signposts telling you where every path will eventually lead you. In the middle of a small rose garden is a wretched concrete pond, empty but for the inch of rainwater that can never be drained from it and the inevitable litter of papers and disintegrating cigarette ends. What else? A spindly copse of pine trees. A kiosk always surrounded by people poring over its meagre display of sweets and cigarettes, paperback novels and ball-point pens. A prefabricated hut nearby in which teas and snacks are served for a few hours every afternoon. The lodge gates through which cars are continually coming and going, under the gaze of a blue-uniformed porter. High brick walls. The main road outside, with some shops and factories in the distance, and traffic always travelling at speed along it. Views from a few places of the immense city filling the horizon to one side, which doesn't seem to give off clouds and fumes, but rather to draw them to itself as inevitably as the rubbish tip in the opposite direction attracts flocks of gulls. Beyond the tip is the usual peri-urban squalor of allotments and railway lines, and beyond them again is a round, coin-like reservoir. The water in it blinks sharply, as if it's been tilted up towards you, whenever the sun shines.

Men and women are always wandering up and down the pathways or circling endlessly in the open spaces: as thoughtful as dons, as indifferent to one another as leaves, as down-at-heel as tramps. Only one or two of the women are always ready to accost strangers and engage them in rambling conversation. The members of staff, in laundered white jackets and trousers, go briskly about their errands. There are always lots of them around. Usually they are good-humoured. Many of them are studying for further qualifications. Even at night, when you get up from bed to go to the lavatory, you are likely to see one of them seated at his desk at the end of the corridor, pen in hand, the lamplight shining on the papers in front of him.

Today, however, the routine was broken for me. I had some visitors. Papa came, together with a girl – curly haired, broad, rather plain – whom I didn't recognise. There were a couple of youngish men with them whom I couldn't place either: neatly dressed fellows, with a professional, faintly vulgar air of detachment from what they were doing. Dr Buchan was also there. Quite a party. One of the young men asked the girl a question which I couldn't overhear. She nodded in reply, looking straight at me in an unfriendly manner. He also asked about a visit which papa (he claimed) had made to me the day before. Again, I didn't catch the answer. They talked together in low voices, Dr Buchan joining in busily. I pricked up my ears when I heard him say something about the writing I had been doing. The young man used the word 'evidence'. Papa became agitated. His voice rose. He began to gesticulate. He said he'd seen some of those papers. I'd shown them to him. There was nothing on them. Nothing to read. Nothing you could make sense of. Just lines and scrawls and scribbles of all kinds – straight lines, crooked lines, wavy lines, zig-zags, criss-crosses, dots, loops, dashes . . . Rubbish. Meaningless stuff. Covering pieces of paper I'd picked up all over the place. Too awful to look at. Especially when you saw how I treasured them.

He was crying. The others gathered around him. In spite of the ridiculous and insulting lies he had just been telling them about my work, I couldn't help feeling sorry for him. He looked so old and shabby. So defeated. To my astonishment I saw Dr Buchan nodding in confirmation of what he'd said. The girl took advantage of the distraction to approach me. She whispered something savagely, her face distorted with rage. I couldn't make out all she was saying, but I caught a name. Susie.

So she'd got at my papers. Somehow. The bitch. The spy. How else could she know about Susie? But not a word had she put in when papa had been carrying on. I looked through her. I wasn't going to give her the satisfaction of a response.

She made a gesture, like a blow she would have liked to strike, before turning away. They all turned to go. The doctor went with them. None of them had said anything to me about how long I am expected to stay in this place, or how I was brought here, or what awaits me when I leave. It's enough to make one despair.

I try not to succumb to it. To despair, I mean. Papa can tell them what he likes. The doctor too. I know what I'm doing. Writing down descriptions of places I have never visited, people I have never met, deeds I have never done, I am a free man. I can honestly say that as long as I have my pen in my hand, I am almost as contented with my lot as Timothy is with his.